The Eyes Have It

Julie Allan

The Eyes Have It
by Julie Allan

...

Copyright ©Palmettos and Pearls Publishing, 2016

PALMETTOS
and PEARLS
PUBLISHING

Palmettos and Pearls Publishing, LLC
Mount Pleasant, SC

Distributed by Bublish, Inc.

Cover Artwork by Berge Design
Publisher's Cataloging-In-Publication Data
(Prepared by The Donohue Group, Inc.)

Names: Allan, Julie, 1968-
Title: The eyes have it / Julie Allan.
Description: Mount Pleasant, SC : Palmettos and Pearls Publishing, LLC,
    [2016] | [Place of distribution not identified] : Bublish, Inc. |
    Series: [Lowcountry home] ; [1] | "A Lowcountry novel"--Cover.
Identifiers: ISBN 978-0-9974875-3-4 | ISBN 0-9974875-3-4
Subjects: LCSH: Divorced women--South Carolina--Fiction. | Restaurants--
    South Carolina--Fiction. | Friendship--Fiction. | Man-woman
    relationships--Fiction. | Chick lit, American. | LCGFT: Domestic
    fiction.
Classification: LCC PS3601.L536 E94 2016 | DDC 813/.6--dc23

Acknowledgments

Just like it takes a village to raise a child, it takes an army of support to take a writer from conception to publishing.

I would like to thank: Kathy, my tireless and knowledgeable, mentor and friend who showed me the way to make this a reality.

To Amy C. and Amy I. who pushed me to just get on with writing. To my wonderful beta readers, Kathleen, Martha and Mary for feedback chapter by chapter.

My grammar gurus, Cindy and Julie.

Chris Berge of Berge Designs for his captivating cover design.

My many friends who have cheered me on and supported me on this journey. I am blessed to have more than I can name.

Finally my parents Mary and Jon, who with love, have always encouraged me to follow my dreams.

Chapter One

The air in the church enveloped Lizzie and Aunt Dorothy with reverence and warmth as they began their solemn journey down the long polished stone aisle. Lizzie gently supported Aunt Dorothy's arm as the two made their way toward the casket sitting just in front of the altar. Self-conscious with so many eyes focused on her, Lizzie concentrated on the limestone below her feet.

Funny, she thought, *I've been up and down this aisle a million times and never noticed all the small bits of fossilized life embedded in this stone. Bits of life frozen in time, just like me.*

Someone coughed. Lizzie looked up. She tried to focus on the task at hand, saying goodbye to Uncle George.

Both women were dressed in modest black dresses, heels and, of course, their pearls. Aunt Dorothy also clutched a linen handkerchief with Uncle George's initials hand-embroidered in the corner. Halfway down the aisle, Lizzie began to drift again, reflecting on the horrific week that had led to this moment.

She couldn't stop reliving it.

On Sunday night, her husband of six years, five months and thirteen days had announced he was in love with his secretary and wanted a divorce.

~

She stared at him across the table, just beyond the perfectly prepared beef tenderloin. He stared back—his eyes dark, cold and beady. *Had they always looked that way?* Lizzie searched her memory. She tried to register what he was saying, but numbness and disbelief overwhelmed her. Perhaps she had misunderstood.

"What did you say?" were the only words she could muster. Without emotion, Mark slowly repeated his divorce declaration. *Really? Could it be more cliché? He's leaving me for his secretary? It's so ... mundane!* Men in movies and books do this to their wives. This just doesn't happen to good southern girls like me. She fought the urge to laugh at the absurdity of it all.

Indignation quickly replaced shock. *I can't believe I gave up my dreams to put you through law school and open your own offices.* She took a deep breath and surveyed the immaculately set table and elegant meal she had prepared. A full glass of 2010 Argentinean Colomé Reserve Malbec stood next to each plate, selected for compatibility. She reached for the stem, took a sip and tossed the wine in Mark's face. In retrospect, it was a complete waste of her favorite vintage.

Mark made a condescending remark about her flair for the dramatic. He ranted about her unworthiness as the wife of an up-and-coming attorney on the fast track for political office.

Apparently she had failed him on all fronts. He continued, reciting a laundry list of faults. Apparently he had regretted marrying her from the beginning. She did loathe the endless cocktail parties, political fundraisers, small talk and endless one-upmanship that defined their social life. She did fully participate, though, always showing up impeccably dressed, with a smile on her face. She played the dutiful, supporting wife well. *Didn't I put aside all of my own dreams to help Mark achieve his? Yes, pretty much from the day we met.* Her brain whirled, desperately trying to make sense of his rejection.

Lizzie sat in utter disbelief as Mark packed his things. *Who is this man I've been sleeping next to all these years?* When she really thought about this, she realized it had been months since she had actually slept next to him. He had slept on the couch, claiming that he'd fallen asleep watching a game or some political talking heads. He had even claimed all-nighters at the office. "Working on a big case," he'd told her. Of course, now she knew *who* the 'big case' involved.

~

She look down again at the limestone and envisioned the toe of her satin shoe peeking out of the silk hem of her bridal dress. She had walked down this same aisle toward Mark. Where Uncle George's casket now sat, they had promised to love and cherish each other for a lifetime. How could she have been so naïve? She remembered the overwhelming nerves, the attempts to calm herself with the thought that this must be how all brides felt. Now, she realized, her entire being was shouting, trying to tell her that she was about to make a huge mistake.

From the moment they were married, Lizzie took her vows seriously. Apparently, this was not the case for Mark. Conveniently, his secretary and newfound love was the niece of a member of Congress, a powerful politician, a real go-getter on the national stage. *I'm much too young to be traded in for a better model. Doesn't this usually happen during men's so-called midlife crisis? Had he ever loved me at all?*

After a mostly sleepless night, Lizzie awoke Monday morning to face work. She prepared for the day in a robot-like fashion, too exhausted and shell-shocked to feel anything. Perhaps today, the job she loathed, the job she had taken so "the love of her life" could open his law firm in Greenville, wouldn't be so bad. Perhaps today, the mundane corporate busywork would occupy her mind and keep her sane. After all, it wasn't a horrible place to work. The people were nice. The work was not demanding. She was more than competent for the job; it just didn't feed her soul. Yes, the place lacked the creativity she craved, but that was okay today. She just needed to keep busy and get through the day.

She'd only been at work an hour, when she headed toward the break room for a second cup of coffee. It was going to be difficult to keep her eyes open for eight hours without regular injections of caffeine. Her boss Leslie walked over.

"Lizzie, would you mind stepping into my office for a moment?"

"Be right there," Lizzie replied.

"Lizzie, you've done fine work since you joined the company. If I had my way, we'd be giving you a raise and a position with more responsibility. However, as you know, we're in the middle of restructuring, and that means budget cuts. I'm sorry to inform you that your job is being eliminated, effective immediately." Leslie droned on about a severance package and how she would be happy to provide references. Lizzie barely heard her. She sat silently on the edge of the chair, a half smile plastered across her face, nodding. *Strike two! What a week!*

Lizzie quickly gathered her personal items, and made a hasty departure. That's just how things worked. One minute you're doing fine work; the next, you're out the door. *Losing income,* she thought, very bad timing. *Leaving a job you hate, not so much. The universe is practically screaming at you to make some changes. You're finally free to find the job you want. Okay, you're unemployed and abandoned. The worst! But now you can go home to Mt. Pleasant and do something you love. There's no reason to stay here in Greenville.*

Bad news always comes in threes, and Lizzie didn't have to wait long for her strike three. On Tuesday morning, after another restless night's sleep, she awoke with no place to go. As she sat staring at the empty side of the closet where Mark's clothes had once been, the phone rang. It was Aunt Dorothy. Uncle George had suffered a stroke and had passed away quietly in his sleep. Could she come home? Aunt Dorothy asked sadly.

Lizzie immediately began to pack—her clothes, her favorite cookbooks, a small collection of novels, a few pieces of art and mementos from her life. She also gathered the belongings of her two golden retrievers, Lucky and Ella. Mark had not wanted to be bothered with dogs until a colleague had pointed out that the press loves stories about politicians and their pets. Though he had acquiesced, they had been Lizzie's dogs from day one. Well, there it all was, sitting by the front door—three boxes and two dogs. *Funny,* she thought, *after clearing out the flotsam and jetsam, most of the things I treasure in life all fit in the back of my SUV.*

On the way out of town she stopped to drop a letter at Mark's office. The note was cold and formal. She was taking the dogs and leaving him the house and all its contents. He could do with it what he wanted. She did not want anything. As soon as he could draw up the divorce papers, she would be glad to sign them. She could be reached at her Aunt Dorothy's back in Mount Pleasant. She was going home.

She had dressed impeccably for this brief visit, sporting a cream linen sheath dress and a gorgeous silver necklace she'd scored at an estate sale. Even if it killed her, she was going to face Mark's secretary with poise and dignity. Delivering the note for Mark, she took a moment to give the naïve Miss Caswell a cool once over, indicating she found her inconsequential. Inside she was dying to leap over the desk and pull out her hair. On the outside, she maintained perfect control, and took a small bit of pleasure in flustering the girl. "Miss Caswell, a little tip. Mark expects his socks folded, not rolled ... and do not use scented fabric softener under any circumstances. I wish you luck, dear, you are going to need it." Lizzie turned and walked away, a little surprised that she'd been able to pull of the snub.

~

The drive back to the coastal town of her childhood was cathartic. As she flew down the interstate, she waffled between euphoria at her newfound freedom thoughts ... and complete panic. *What the hell am I going to do with the rest of my life! Lizzie, stay calm. First things first. Aunt Dorothy needs you.*

Aunt Dorothy and Uncle George had taken Lizzie in at five years old when her own parents had been killed in a car accident coming home from a local baseball game. Aunt Dorothy was daddy's big sister by ten years, and she and Uncle George never had children of their own. They lived in the Old Village section of Mount Pleasant in a coastal cottage with wide porches and cypress floors. The back porch looked out over the Charleston Harbor, Fort Sumter and beyond to the tip of James Island and Folly Beach.

Lizzie had spent hours in the shade of the yard, where towering live oaks, dripping in Spanish moss, led down to a crab dock on the Harbor. Aunt Dorothy and Uncle George had loved Lizzie as their own daughter. She had even been legally adopted by them, so she could take their last name of Long. She could hardly wait to rid her life of Hargrove, and legally enjoy her real last name again.

Her childhood had been idyllic with the Longs. Uncle George had taught her to fish and crab and shrimp—to appreciate the many gifts of a coastal lifestyle. He loved the outdoors, and had passed along that love to Lizzie. She had worked beside him in the garden. Aunt Dorothy had taught her to cook and bake, skills that had grown into an art form and passion for Lizzie. So many fond memories of canning the harvest from the garden, making pickles and cooking lots of dishes with the shrimp and crab she and Uncle George would bring back from their outings. At one time in her life, she'd dreamed of turning her love of fresh, Lowcountry food into a career. Mark's ambition had sidelined that goal.

Lizzie pondered how her marriage had led to her isolation from so many of the people and activities she loved. Mark and his friends turned up their noses at anyone who did not fit their shallow mold. She'd given up more than she realized. Luckily, she'd managed to keep up her reading, another gift Aunt Dorothy had bestowed upon her—a way to inspire a love of learning and curiosity about the world. Ironically, books had been Lizzie's steady companion during all those nights that her husband had not managed to find his way to their bed.

How happy she was to be home, even if under the saddest of circumstances. She had missed Mount Pleasant during the years she had followed Mark, first to Columbia for law school, then to Greenville as he began his career. How many times had he promised her they would come back to Mount Pleasant—as soon as he finished school, as soon as he'd established a name for himself. Then again, he'd promised so many things—babies to come after he graduated, a future of Junior League meetings and serving as the PTA mom. Nothing would have made her happier, but when they'd arrived in Greenville he complained that he was under too much pressure to add fatherhood to his responsibilities. Weeks turned into months, then years. Mark dictated all the decisions in their lives—how she spent her time outside work, who she could befriend, where and with whom they socialized. Everything was focused on cultivating connections for his career. She realized that besides a few people from work, there were no friends to miss in Greenville. At age twenty-eight, Lizzie was being forced to push the reset button. As she thought about this, she found herself becoming angry—angry with Mark, angry with Miss Caswell, and if she was being totally honest, angry with herself.

As she pulled into the driveway, she could see Aunt Dorothy sitting on the joggling board by the front door. *Always a pillar of strength, my Aunt Dorothy, an anchor of serenity and reason.* Walking toward the porch, Lizzie detected in her beloved aunt a new frailty. The grief of losing Uncle George was etched across her face, revealing the shattering blow to her heart. Seeing her aunt this way shook Lizzie to her core. *Aunt Dorothy, you are my rock. How can I find my way if my beacon has lost its light?* When Lizzie reached the top of the steps, she looked in her aunt's eyes and was relieved to still see a familiar sparkle still there. They embraced, and in that moment Lizzie realized that somehow it was all going to be okay.

~

As they reached the casket of Uncle George together, Aunt Dorothy and Lizzie squeezed hands and bowed their heads. The church, filled to capacity with mourners, was completely silent. It was the most solemn of moments, broken suddenly by the sound of a marble dropping onto the limestone floor. Lizzie opened her eyes just in time to see Aunt Dorothy's piercing blue glass eyeball roll between their legs and come to a stop, pupil facing up, at the feet of Mrs. Marie McGantry, who was sitting in the front pew.

Mrs. McGantry let out an ear-splitting scream, and several people gasped, "Oh my God!" Lizzie and the Right Reverend Christian Truett scrambled toward Mrs. McGantry and the roving eye, as hundreds of horrified mourners looked on.

While Lizzie crouched down to locate the eyeball, Reverend Truett escorted Mrs. McGantry to the parish hall where she could compose herself. Aunt Dorothy, for her part, turned towards the crowd with her hand covering her missing eye. With a jovial laugh, she declared that George would have enjoyed some excitement to liven up his funeral. The gathered mourners smiled and relaxed. Even in her grief, Aunt Dorothy's signature humor and grace were evident. As Lizzie reached towards the glass orb under the pew, a large tanned hand with long elegant fingers grasped it. Lizzie rose slowly, and found herself face-to-face with her old high school sweetheart, Bennett Wilson. His eyes danced with amusement as she managed to mumble, "Nice of you to come," before snatching up the eyeball and retreating with Aunt Dorothy to the safety of their family pew.

Unceremoniously, Aunt Dorothy wiped off the eyeball with her hemstitched hanky and plopped it back into its socket. She winked at Reverend Truett, who had returned to the altar. He cleared his throat and went on with the service, barely missing a beat.

Despite the eyeball fiasco, it was a lovely service. Many people spoke, honoring Uncle George for being an outstanding member of the community, a warden of the church and an active member of the Rotary Club for many years. They talked about his patience with children, his years as a tee-ball coach. It seemed he'd taught every child in the Old Village to shrimp, crab and fish. People reminisced about his wicked sense of humor, like the time he had dressed up as Julia Child and did a mock cooking demonstration in the church Fundraising Follies one year. Many talked about the unfailing devotion he had for his two girls, Dorothy and Lizzie.

Finally, Aunt Dorothy stood up and told the crowd that this was not to be a day of sadness, but one of celebration. George's was the epitome of a life well-lived and free of pretense. She invited everyone back to the house for a Lowcountry boil and libations. Mrs. McGantry, now back in her pew shot Dorothy a look of disapproval. She believed in traditional tea sandwiches and light refreshments in the parish hall were more appropriate after a funeral gathering. She did, however, encouraged her fellow mourners to sing George's favorite hymn, "Amazing Grace" with gusto. The congregation was happy to oblige, and Lizzie and her aunt followed the casket out of the church to the enthusiastic sound.

After a short ritual at the gravesite, Lizzie and Dorothy returned to the house to greet their guests and celebrate the life of George William Long in a manner he would have greatly approved. Folks made themselves at home and pitched in to set out the food and drinks. Lizzie hugged hundreds of people, many whom she had not seen since her wedding. No one asked about Mark. *Did they know ... or did they just not like him?*

It was a blessing to see so many rally around Aunt Dorothy. This was the sense of community that she had so desperately missed while she was away. She was glad that Aunt Dorothy had said she could stay as long as she needed. It would be good for both of them.

Chapter Two

Bang, bang, bang ... Lizzie woke up with a start. The hot Carolina sun was streaming through the salt glazed glass of her childhood bedroom. Lizzie cracked open one eye as she felt two noses snuffling her feet, Lucky's tail thumping out good morning against the foot of the bed. Her eyes widened and she sat straight up as wavy black hair and a pair of startling but very familiar blue-green eyes peered into the second floor window. "What the heck!" Lizzie exclaimed as she leapt up indignantly and threw up the sash demanding an explanation. Bennett shot her a practiced "get a grip" expression and slowly eyed her from her bare feet up to the top of her bed-head hair. For a moment they stood there, staring each other down as the humid salty air stirred lazily around them. Lizzie could smell the pluff mud, *it must be low tide,* she thought.

Suddenly Lizzie was self-conscious that she was standing there in nothing but an old t-shirt she had dug out of a drawer the night before, *note to self, do laundry today* she thought. Thank goodness the shirt was baggy and came down to her knees.

"Isn't that one of my old shirts?" asked Bennett, noting the large size and the logo for the Windjammer, a favorite place to hang-out on the Isle of Palms.

"I don't know, I found it at the bottom of a drawer," Lizzie answered, blushing three shades of scarlet as she remembered it was one she had neglected to return to him ten years before when they had broken up. "It's beside the point," she continued, "this is a new low for you Bennett Wilson, just what do you think you're doing, spying in my window?" Before Bennett could answer, Lizzie could hear Aunt Dorothy calling up from the yard.

"Bennett dear, when you finish with the shutter, come on in the kitchen. There is a fresh pot of coffee and some biscuits ready to come out of the oven. Oh, and tell Miss Lizzie it is well past rise and shine time and I need to fill her in on the plans for the day."

"I believe you heard the lady, you best get yourself presentable and report downstairs," Bennett said, thoroughly enjoying Lizzie's discomfort.

Avoiding meeting Bennett's gaze Lizzie shut the window and quickly drew the curtains. For a moment she stood there seething with indignation, but as the dogs danced around her legs, anxious to get out to the yard, she pulled herself back into control. After splashing some cold water on her face and brushing her teeth, she quickly pulled on a pair of shorts and her favorite bridge run t-shirt. She brushed her long blond hair back in a ponytail and headed down the stairs greeted by the tantalizing aromas that were emanating from the kitchen. She let Lucky and Ella out the back door and turned to face Aunt Dorothy who was opening a fresh jar of her strawberry preserves.

With a wistful look on her face, Aunt Dorothy set in to give Lizzie a "talking to." She reminded Lizzie it had been a month since the funeral, since she had lost her job and her marriage had finally crumbled, perhaps it was time to give up the pity party, stop moping about and find a new path. After all, hadn't she lost her own husband, did Lizzie see her moping? No, ma'am, she had not even missed her weekly shift volunteering at the library. Lizzie began to protest the idea she had been indulging in a pity party but snapped shut as the door opened and Lucky and Ella came bounding in, tails wagging and escorting Bennett into the kitchen.

"Come sit Bennett, the biscuits just came out of the oven." Aunt Dorothy smiled as Lizzie glared across the room at her.

But Lizzie also came obediently to the table, taking care to sit the farthest from Bennett as possible. She suspected Aunt Dorothy in a loving but misguided way was trying to finagle a renewal of their adolescent romance. Lizzie wanted nothing of it; she was still smarting from the break with Mark, really not the losing of him but the idea that their marriage had failed for all to see. And Bennett of all people ... what could Aunt Dorothy be thinking, he didn't even seem to be gainfully employed. Since she had been home she found herself running into him around town, and he was always in shorts, Guy Harvey t-shirts and flip flops like he had just gotten off a boat. Here he was, fixing shutters for Aunt Dorothy. He apparently did odd jobs to eke out a living while he spent the bulk of his time playing. As Lizzie sat sullenly spreading the silky preserves onto the flaky biscuit with a pool of melted butter beginning to escape over its edge, she had gathered from the conversation between Bennett and Aunt Dorothy this was not the first job he had done around there. Last spring he had apparently helped Uncle George replace rotting wood on the porches and he had been taking care of the yard for a good part of the last year. *I wonder how much Dorothy is paying him,* Lizzie wondered, *note to self, ask and also tell her I will take on the yard, help to save a buck,* she thought. With Uncle George gone Aunt Dorothy would need to economize.

"Lizzie dear, where are your manners? Bennett just asked you a question and you ignored him." Aunt Dorothy said with a rare air of disapproval.

Lizzie snapped back to attention, "Um ... what did you say?" Bennett's eye seemed to cloud with concern, or was that pity for the shambles her life was in?

"I was asking are you staying long, or are you going to go back to Greenville?" Bennett repeated.

Lizzie gave an involuntary shudder as Mark's self-important smirk and beady soulless eyes flashed in her brain. "Oh, I don't know, I want to go to the reading of the will and help Aunt Dorothy get settled," She replied, deliberately vague.

Dorothy smiled and reached over patting Lizzie's hand. "Well dear, I wanted to make sure you didn't make any plans for this afternoon. We need to be at the lawyer's office at two today."

"No worries, no plans," Lizzie flippantly answered. Bennett pushed back from the table. "Thank you Miz Long, your biscuits are heaven and your company divine," he murmured as he gently took Aunt Dorothy's hand and raised it to his lips.

Lizzie rolled her eyes, but Aunt Dorothy clearly tickled, beamed at Bennett and replied, "Now Bennett, how many times have I told you to call me Aunt Dorothy. You are just like family after all," and as she said it she shot Lizzie a look as if to say and you could have made that a reality child.

Lizzie rolled her eyes again. "See you around Bennett; I'm sure you have other jobs to get to."

Bennett looked at Lizzie quizzically but simply replied, "See you around Lizzie." He gave Lucky and Ella a quick pat and headed out the door.

Aunt Dorothy turned to Lizzie, "You could be a little more gracious to Bennett, child. After all he has done a lot around here for both me and your Uncle George."

"Speaking of that, how much do you pay him for the work he does around here?"

"Pay him? My goodness Lizzie, we don't pay him. Bennett has helped out around here out of the goodness of his heart. Did you not know how close he and Uncle George have been, why it's like Bennett was his son-in-law! Honestly Lizzie I don't understand how you became so judgmental and quick to jump to conclusions about other people, I know your Uncle George and I taught you better than that!" Aunt Dorothy chided.

Lizzie cheeks burned. She seemed to be disappointing everyone in her life. Before Lizzie could respond, the phone rang and Aunt Dorothy was swept up in an animated conversation with her best friend and old college roommate Maggie. Maggie, who had lost her husband a few years before, she would be a good one to guide Aunt Dorothy through her grief. Lizzie carefully rinsed off the dishes and put away the preserves as she mused over the news that Bennett did things for her family out of the supposed goodness of his heart. *So what did he do for a living? Was he seeing anyone?* Lizzie blushed and chided herself for even wondering about Bennett. They had parted ways at eighteen, off to different colleges and different lives. Hadn't she been confident in what her future would be? Lizzie as wife, mother, her own business utilizing her culinary passion ... while Bennett had been lacking direction and ambition. How had the decade that had passed shaped them? Lizzie didn't know what had happened to Bennett, although she assumed he was still lacking direction. Unfortunately, she did know what had happened to her. She had been sucked into the charming but arrogant life of Mark Harris Hargrove the Third and been convinced her dreams were expendable. After all he had a five year plan, ambition, and even suggested she might be first lady of the state if he attained his political aspirations of which he had no doubt. Lizzie shuddered again, who had she become and where was the girl she had been? If she was honest she had to admit it was not surprising to find out that Bennett had continued a relationship with her family or that he had helped out on a regular basis. Bennett was always one to help from the time they were kids. Had he been a Boy Scout he would have epitomized the creed to serve others. Uncle George and Aunt Dorothy had always loved him and were crushed when Lizzie had broken things off. Bennett got along well with all kinds of people, young and old, well-off and the less fortunate. He was so different from Mark. Mark had been all about the "right people." If you did not have something to advance him and his plan, then he would not waste his time cultivating a relationship.

It made Lizzie wonder why he had picked her to marry in the first place. Her mind flashed to a moment just a few days after their honeymoon. They were packing up to head to Columbia for Law school and she had been surprised by Mark's reaction when Uncle George had informed him, Lizzie's inheritance from her parents had been spent on raising her and paying for her college education. Now that she was looking back she realized Mark was a bit angry. He had assumed she had a pile of life insurance money that would pay for his grand plan to become a future state senator or governor. Shortly after that he pushed her into corporate work, claiming her income was needed to fund their future. After all he was working hard at school for the same purpose. *How could I have been so blind to his motivations, his character? What does that say about my character that I blindly followed him, took direction from him and even began to filter the world through his criteria?* She mused.

She called to Lucky and Ella to walk down to the dock with her. She was going to look for crabs, stare at the marsh grasses and the water beyond. She had worked herself up and the familiar sights, sounds and smells of the low-country marsh and the harbor beyond were a proven elixir to help her organize her thoughts. She sat on the end of the dock and watched the water and sun dance together. On the sandbar across the way a pair of pelicans perched.

In the distance she could see a sailboat heading out into the harbor. These were all familiar sights and that grounded Lizzie. She felt the stress leach out of her pores with the sweat the humid air created. As she relaxed she allowed her mind to concede that Aunt Dorothy was right, she had been moping. It was time to face the reality of her life. She was ending her marriage. She was unemployed. These facts were complicated by the grief she was marinating in over Uncle George. The reappearance of Bennett in her life was confusing and the fact that feelings for him stirred easily was disconcerting. While she knew she had to deal with her own circumstances and figure out what her new path would be she also realized she was embarrassingly self-absorbed. In her defense she had spent the last few years on auto-pilot, not dwelling on her feelings or examining her life, if she had, she might have left Mark before he left her. She was making up for lost time, reflection was the only way she could figure out how she got here. Still, she needed to do a better job at balancing this self-discovery with the needs of Aunt Dorothy. Had she not told herself on the drive from Greenville to Mount Pleasant that Aunt Dorothy came first? Today would be another step in that process as the family lawyer, Thomas Lee, a life-long friend, whom Aunt Dorothy and Uncle George affectionately called Tommy. Mr. Lee would handle the official reading of the will and various other legal chores to tidy up the affairs of Uncle George.

Lizzie sighed. She could stay on the dock all afternoon, but it was time to change into more appropriate attire and turn her attentions to the care of Aunt Dorothy. The dogs had long since lost interest in the goings-on on the dock and were laying in the shade waiting on Lizzie to let them back in so they could nap on the cool wood floor for the afternoon. Lizzie got Lucky and Ella some fresh water and then went to see if Aunt Dorothy would like her to fix a little lunch.

Aunt Dorothy was grateful for the suggestion and sat at the kitchen table while Lizzie whipped up some BLT's and got out some of the homemade pickled okra that always seemed to be on hand.

"I'm sorry if I came down on you a little hard this morning child, I just want you to find your happiness." Aunt Dorothy said while Lizzie turned the sizzling bacon in the pan. The aroma had brought the dogs in, ever hopeful a morsel might drop to the floor.

"Yes, ma'am, I know and I have to admit I was wallowing. Uncle George would not have approved of that. Besides I promised I would be here for you, so do not worry about me, I will find my way. After all my Long upbringing won't allow me to do anything but," Lizzie replied as she slathered Duke's mayonnaise on slices of bread.

She quickly assembled the sandwiches with ripe sliced tomatoes, crisp lettuce and smoky bacon; it was like summer simplicity on a plate. After a delightful lunch where both women took care to keep the conversation light and jovial, they both changed into summer dresses and put on their pearls. It was time for the reading of the will.

Chapter Three

Lizzie and Aunt Dorothy sat side by side in the two leather wing-backed chairs in front of the polished mahogany desk of Mr. Thomas Lee, Attorney at Law and longtime family friend of the Longs. An intern had offered them each a bottled water and they each clutched the bottles as if they were the last of the water reserves on Earth. Aunt Dorothy uncharacteristically sat twisting the cap on and off. She was not usually nervous, but the finality of reading the will had unsettled her. Luckily she was very comfortable with Mr. Lee. In fact, Uncle George and Mr. Lee had been friends since their first day of grade school. So when Mr. Lee entered the room in his seersucker suit and his perky bow tie festooned with palmetto trees, it came to no one's surprise when he bent down and tenderly kissed Aunt Dorothy's cheek and gave Lizzie an affectionate pat on the head.

"Sorry to keep you lovely ladies waiting. I was just finishing the additional project you called me about last week Dorothy." He said as he rounded the corner of his desk and settled into his chair. "Now to the business at hand, as you know the bulk of George's estate passes automatically to you, Dorothy, but he did have some special wishes he wanted to see carried out. First, he left a gift of one-hundred thousand dollars to the Park and Recreation department of the town of Mount Pleasant to fund uniforms and registration fees etc. for youth in our community who could otherwise not afford such fees; the fund will be managed and invested by my office so that it will be a gift that will continue on for years to come."

"But," interjected Lizzie in protest, "how can Aunt Dorothy afford to give up such a large amount of money?" "Oh, my dear, one-hundred thousand is just a drop in the bucket when we are talking about the accounts of your Uncle George and Aunt Dorothy," laughed Mr. Lee.

Lizzie sat stunned, her mind whirring through a flash of memories. Uncle George reusing bits of string and other things he saved and salvaged. Aunt Dorothy canning and preserving home grown or picked at Boone Farms fruits and vegetables. The comfortable but un-ostentatious life they had lived. *How in the world could they have large bank accounts?* When Lizzie thought back to her upbringing, she had not wanted for anything, but she was not spoiled by any means. She babysat in the neighborhood to supplement her wants and as a teenager had waitressed to help pay for a used car. At one time she had made homemade biscuits and preserves and sold them as boxed sets around the neighborhood to fund a new surfboard.

Uncle George had always paid for things she needed and even some of the things she wanted, but they had not been materialistic and Lizzie in turn had not been either. In fact she had been downright uncomfortable with Mark's obsession with driving the "right" car, wearing designer labels and being seen at the most popular restaurants and bars. Lizzie had become a bit of a clothes horse during her marriage. She enjoyed quality, classic clothing as most southern women did, but she had never gotten hung up on labels like he did. She had always assumed Uncle George and Aunt Dorothy had a modest income. She could not remember a time that they had even discussed money, other than being responsible with it and also the importance of giving to the church and other philanthropic causes.

"Now to the church," Mr. Lee was saying and he continued on naming a few more special donations he wanted named. "Now Dorothy, that leaves you with a remaining estate valued at over ten million dollars. I am assuming you want to continue to have it managed as it has been."

"Why, yes, Tommy," answered Aunt Dorothy, although I do plan to make a substantial withdrawal in the next few weeks as my best friend Maggie and I finalize our plans."

"George would definitely approve," replied Mr. Lee as if he knew exactly what Aunt Dorothy was referring to. Lizzie felt a tinge of jealousy and bewilderment as she realized she was in the dark about a lot of things. *What plans could Aunt Dorothy have with Maggie and what did she consider to be a substantial amount?* mused Lizzie.

It was obvious to her that Mr. Lee had been involved in the managing of Uncle George and Aunt Dorothy's affairs for a long time and he was trusted with that responsibility. He also seemed privy to what Aunt Dorothy planned to do as she adjusted to her new role of widow. *Why hasn't Aunt Dorothy trusted me with this knowledge? Why did Uncle George and Aunt Dorothy hide their affluence from me?* Questions began to swirl in her mind again. *Did they really hide it, or was I so self-absorbed I never noticed.* For certain she had never thought to ask, and it would have seemed poor manners to inquire even if the thought had crossed her mind. Still ten million dollars! Uncle George must have been a master at investing. He certainly had been a master at saving.

Turning to Lizzie, Mr. Lee gazed at her with genuine affection and said, "Lizzie, we have several items of business to discuss. The first is moving you forward in your divorce from Mark. He signed the legal separation papers and they are ready for you to sign, as you know there will be a one year waiting period. If you want to go after him for his infidelity … we can seek a financial settlement. I did some preliminary research and I have discovered his so called fledgling law practice is clearing him a six figure salary."

"WHAT!" Lizzie practically choked on her words. "That son of a …" and she glanced sheepishly at Aunt Dorothy.

"… Of a wicked witch" finished Aunt Dorothy.

"To think I worked that boring job to pay our mortgage and cover our expenses. Hell, I even rinsed out Ziploc bags to reuse and take my lunch in." Lizzie ranted. How did he hide his finances from her, his wife! How was I blind to it all? Lizzie felt her brain ache with the pressure.

Aunt Dorothy gently laid a cool hand against Lizzie's cheek, "Child, the past is gone, today is here and the future is what we make of it." Aunt Dorothy had been saying that to her for years, every time she had imploded over a real or imagined wrong.

Lizzie took a deep breath and looked directly at Mr. Lee, "Mark is my past and the sooner we make that fact legal the better. I left with all that was of value to me and I don't want to drag these procedures out. He can keep his six figures and his politically connected girlfriend. I want a clean break and a fresh start."

"I am tickled pink to hear that," said Aunt Dorothy, "So, Tommy, I think it is time we let her in on some of the other business at hand."

"Ah, yes, so as you are already aware in the event of both Dorothy and George passing the entire Long estate would pass to you, and as Dorothy is still alive, that day will God willing, be far in the future. However at the time of your parent's passing a small estate and a life insurance pay-out were held in your name and to be managed by your Uncle George, and as you have gathered from the revelations this afternoon, combined with a careful lifestyle and a gift of making investments grow, that modest sum has bloomed into a significant amount."

Lizzie interrupted, "I thought that money had been spent to raise me and pay for my education? How come when I married Mark, Uncle George did not give me the funds then? Did he not trust me?" The questions spilled from her.

"Perhaps I should answer that," Aunt Dorothy said in a soothing voice. "You see child, your Uncle George and frankly myself as well, we found Mark to be ... to be, well a little lacking in character and we were concerned he would find a way to separate you from your money. We kind of knew or at least hoped that one day you would realize the kind of man he is and well, divorce him like you are doing now."

Lizzie stared at Aunt Dorothy in disbelief. "How come you never said anything? How could you stand by and watch me marry Mark?" she asked.

"It wasn't our place to chart your path. You came home from college and proclaimed how perfect he was and how much you loved him and described your future life with him with such certainty we knew you would not listen to us, but we did know we could protect your interests and had it worked out eventually we would have given you the funds," Aunt Dorothy answered assertively.

Lizzie sat back in her chair and tried to let the overload of information sink in. "Just how much is this significant amount?" she asked.

"In the ballpark of three and a half mill, give or take a few thou. You should know, legally, George had discretion to hold and manage these funds for you until your thirtieth birthday at which time they would have been released to you."

Lizzie felt dizzy and hot. Aunt Dorothy handed her a fresh bottle of water and one of her ever-present hemstitched hankies. It was a little more than Lizzie could absorb. "I think I need some air, when we finish here I am going to head out and take a long walk on the beach if that is okay with you, Aunt Dorothy?"

"That's a fine idea, but you will need to drop me back at the house first."

"I need you to sign the separation agreement before you leave, so sometime next week we can sign the financial documents turning the funds over to you. Although I would advise you to have them managed as they have been and use them as you need them. The separation agreement needs to be in place first to protect you from Mark making any claims on your financial windfall." Mr. Lee handed Lizzie a pen.

"Fine," Lizzie said tersely and snatched up the pen and with a flourish, signed the papers.

As they made their goodbyes, Mr. Lee hugged Lizzie and whispered in her ear, "George and Dorothy have always had your best interests at heart. Go easy on Dorothy for keeping all this from you."

Lizzie gave him a weak smile and replied, "I will." "Now, Tommy, you need to come by next week to have supper with us. We have one more matter to discuss and no worries, Lizzie, this matter has nothing to do with decisions made in the past. But rather a plan for the future." And with that Aunt Dorothy turned on her heel and headed out to the car.

Lizzie knew the sooner she got Aunt Dorothy home, the sooner she could head out to the Isle of Palms and take that walk at the beach. She would need to sort through all Aunt Dorothy and Tommy had thrown at her this afternoon.

When Lizzie and Aunt Dorothy pulled in the driveway, Aunt Dorothy reached out her hand and gently laid it on Lizzie's arm. "Lizzie, I know the information you heard today has you confused and possibly made you a little angry with Uncle George and myself, but you must know how much we love you, and that all our decisions, right or wrong, have always been guided by that" Aunt Dorothy said.

Her eyes welled with tears and Lizzie leaned over to give Aunt Dorothy a kiss on the cheek. "That is something I have always been sure of," she replied.

Lizzie got Aunt Dorothy settled, took the dogs out, and then changed into shorts and a tank top. Slipping on her favorite flip flops, she headed out to the Isle of Palms; she needed the sound of the surf and the feel of the sand at her feet to help her sort through the hurricane of thoughts that refused to quiet down. The beach— another reason to love the lowcountry, another reason to be glad to be back home.

⁓

She took the Ben Sawyer Bridge onto Sullivan's Island then turned left, passing many of the charming beach cottages that had survived storms big and small. She crossed Breach Inlet and smiled as she spied the great expanse of ocean on one side and the Inter-coastal Waterway on the other. This took her on to the Isle of Palms and she could take the connector home. It took some time to find parking along the business district strip as the summer season was in full swing, finally getting a spot near the Windjammer. She fed the meter begrudgingly, remembering when the parking was free. Taking her keys and a bottle of water she headed out to the sand.

Chapter Four

Lizzie plopped down on the sand and glanced back the way she had come. She sat her flip flops down next to her and sighed. She had parked down near the fishing pier and walked all the way down to 34th Avenue. It was going to be a long walk back to the car. There were a few families playing on the beach, most likely vacationers renting the houses along this section of the Isle of Palms. She found herself feeling a little wistful as she observed a young mom coaxing her toddler to explore the surf as the water came in and pulled back in a rhythmic pattern.

She had wanted a family so badly. She and Mark had many an argument about when to start a family. Looking back she could see he kept putting her off because he was actively looking for someone more suitable, someone more successful or someone politically connected and most likely wealthy, to be the mother of his children. Thank goodness they had not had any children. She could not imagine having to be tied to him forever, or even how those children would turn out with his alternative set of values, so different from the ones she was raised with. Her mind quieted and she brought her focus back to the water.

The few surfers sitting on their boards beyond the breakers, were patiently watching the swells. She could tell they were locals. How did she know? It had been just a decade before when she would have been among them. Isle of Palms was not known for surfing like the washout on Folly Beach and to serious surfers the wave action on Isle of Palms was laughable, but for Lizzie some of her most idyllic summer memories as a teenager had been hanging out on her board with Bennett and their friends riding the baby waves and believing life would always be that easy. Of course there were times, especially if a hurricane lurked off shore that the waves could grow to be quite powerful. At those times they would come out seeking the thrill of the challenge despite their parents' fears of the danger the pre-storm waves brought.

Now as Lizzie reflected on those days she realized her life had become like those challenging waves fraught with riptides and she longed to return to the gentle swells of happier times. Today the surf was one to two feet and the sound of the breakers was soothing, like a white noise machine.

She forced her mind to turn to the end of her marriage. *How could Mark have been so dishonest with me?* He had hidden his income and had manipulated her. Not just since law school, but if she was honest with herself since the day they had met as undergrads. She had been swayed by his swaggering self-confidence, which she now recognized as pure arrogance. He had seen in her someone who would put his needs first. *Wasn't I raised to care for others? When did that come to mean I had to deny my own desires? How did I get to this place? Surely there had been some happy times.*

But as she thought back, even the so called happy moments had been marred by his arrogant and demanding ways. At their own wedding he had been more concerned that the photographer captured the "right" guests than interacting with her friends and family. It was not just the end of her marriage that weighed heavily on her mind. *How could I have not known that Uncle George and Aunt Dorothy were so financially stable?* She had just made assumptions based on what she had observed, how they had lived their lives.

SMACK, Lizzie's brain registered the truth of the matter—she was guilty of assuming and she could hear Bennett saying, "You know assume makes an ass out of u and me." *Had he been aware of my shallow tendencies even way back when?* The questions continued to whir through her like the off-shore wind that buffeted her skin. *How come Uncle George never told me his concerns about Mark? I would have listened! No I wouldn't have, she admitted sheepishly. I was so sure!*

Apparently the truth of how she came to be in her current circumstances rested squarely on her shoulders. That was what galled her the most—had she just looked a little deeper, relied on the values instilled by Uncle George and Aunt Dorothy, her life would be entirely different. She heard the echo of Aunt Dorothy in her mind, *the past is past, the present is here and the future is what we make of it.*

Maybe to turn things around she needed to get away from dwelling on the past. Some questions she needed to ponder and face the hard answers, but wringing her hands over what was done would not help her move forward. What would her life look like had she made other decisions? For one thing she would not have married Mark. She would have returned to Mount Pleasant after college, she might have even married Bennett and started a family. That thought made her face feel hot. She definitely would have pursued a career of her own interest, something that would have fed her soul. That was definitely something she could change moving forward. She also couldn't deny her work in the business world would make her savvier if she decided to pursue her own business. So she could not write off all her experiences during her marriage as being a waste.

She began to formulate a vision of her own business. She could see cooking and baking, incorporating in the abundance of food that came from the farm and the sea right here in her own community. She would need to talk her ideas over with Aunt Dorothy. Maybe she should call M.A. her childhood friend officially named Mary Ann, but her close friends and family had long ago shortened it. With Lizzie in Greenville and M.A. in Richmond along with her husband, daughters and nursing career, they had drifted apart. No ... she was feeling too vulnerable to call M.A., sure that M.A. would not understand. After all she was happy, she had children, and she had a career she loved.

Lizzie stop it, you are self-doubting again, what did you let Mark turn you into? She chided herself. One thing M.A. was not was judgmental. But she had not even called M.A. after Mark had announced he wanted a divorce. Nor had she called her when she had learned about Uncle George. *Why was that?* It was not because she did not want to share her life with M.A, it was more that she was in shock. Lizzie had been on autopilot. She wasn't even sure how she had managed to get out of Greenville with all her important possessions. After the funeral, she had wallowed. She was sure M.A. had heard what had happened so why hadn't she called? She did send Aunt Dorothy a beautiful hydrangea and a loving card addressed to them both. Maybe this week she should try to call. It would be good to talk things over with her.

Lizzie felt cold despite the warm breeze that stirred around her. She liked to think it was Mark's fault that she was isolated from her friends but the truth of the matter was she was equally to blame. She could have maintained her friendships despite Mark's efforts to leave them behind. She could have stood up to his snide remarks about the important people in her life. Somewhere along the way she had lost her backbone. She could not pinpoint the exact moment, it had been a subtle manipulation on Mark's part, but she had let it happen. She felt anger stir up within. What was that song by Sting, which had that line ... "she can be all four seasons in one day." Lizzie's barometer fluctuated from sadness to anger, to confusion, to giddiness. It was mentally draining and she needed to find a way to stabilize things soon.

She dug her toes into the wet sand and became aware of a shadow blocking out the sun. Shielding her eyes with her hands she looked up to see Bennett standing there holding his surf board, glistening from the salty drops that clung to his skin.

"Hey Lizzie, should-a brought your board, it would be like old times."

"If only it could be that simple, to go back to that time I mean, she answered."

Bennett sat down in the sand next to her and without even saying a word somehow he prompted Lizzie to spill her secrets, just like he had done when they were kids. She talked for the good part of an hour and Bennett just listened as she told him all about Mark and how their marriage was ending and why, the surprises she had learned at Mr. Lee's office about Uncle George and Aunt Dorothy and even the doubts she had about her own judgment and confusion about what to do now.

When she'd finally been quiet for a few minutes Bennett spoke, "Well, the way I see it Lizzie, you have a rare opportunity. This is a chance to make a new life for yourself and with little baggage from your mistakes. You don't have kids and you have funds to pursue your dreams. All you have to do is figure out what that dream is and this time remember to be less dazzled by the packaging and pay more attention to the content."

Lizzie felt her face grow hot as she listened to Bennett's judgment. Who was he to lecture her about being successful and accuse her of being shallow? Well, okay so she had come to that conclusion herself, but it was somewhat more painful to hear it from someone else.

Lizzie found she could not look Bennett in the eye, which was a shame for had she had the courage she would have found genuine affection looking back at her, giving her support and willing her to succeed in getting her life back together. Instead she scrambled to her feet and mumbled she was late getting back. She quickly started back towards the fishing pier and for a long way she could feel Bennett's eyes burning into her back, imagining his scorn for her choices, not realizing his relief that in fact she had finally come to her senses.

The walk back was indeed long and she distracted herself with people-watching as she moved along. The beach was definitely a place where people let it all hang out. She saw corpulent souls in bitty pieces of Spandex. There were shapely folks who flaunted what they had. All looking content with life. That was the balm the beach gave—it didn't matter what life was like off the sand, on the sand you were free, transported back to sandcastle and Popsicle days. The endorphins from the sun and the soothing lullaby of the waves was healing. She found herself imagining lives for these strangers that made her own look fairy tale worthy.

Despite her heavy mood she found herself smiling. She had walked and played on this beach since before she could remember and she was back here with no reason to leave. Maybe Bennett was right—maybe she should focus on the good fortune her upheaval had actually revealed. She resolved to look forward. Bennett ... he had sat and listened to her like old times and her heart ached as she thought of the friendship they had lost when they had ended their romance. *Maybe the friendship was salvageable?* It was a comforting thought.

As she brushed the sand off her feet and got into the car, she turned her thoughts to a vision of what her future, at least her future work life, would look like. It built from the spark of an idea she had contemplated in the sand. She became anxious to share her idea with Aunt Dorothy. As the early evening sunshine cast a saturated glow over the marshes she crossed the bridge over the Inter-Coastal Waterway and headed back to the house.

~

Aunt Dorothy was lounging on the hanging bed swing on the back porch looking over some brochures and travel magazines.

"Going somewhere?" queried Lizzie as she handed Aunt Dorothy a fresh glass of iced tea.

"Thinking about it," Aunt Dorothy answered, not volunteering any details.

Lizzie decided to leave the topic alone for now. She had her own conversation she needed to have, but how to start?

"Did you have a productive walk on the beach?"

That gave Lizzie an opening and she shared with Dorothy her encounter with Bennett, minus the judgment, and shared with her the idea of how to re-launch her life.

Aunt Dorothy listened attentively and when Lizzie finished she said. "Now child, that sounds like the real Lizzie Long. I can't see how it can be anything but successful. If you are sure this is what you want to do, I know Tommy can help. Let's get Tommy over here so we can get you started."

"I am so glad that you like the idea!" Lizzie said and she felt her spirits rising.

"Bennett would be glad to help too," added Aunt Dorothy.

Lizzie rolled her eyes. "Nice try, but I can't imagine how Bennett could help; besides I need to prove I can stand on my own two feet with this." Lizzie sassed.

"Oh, I think you might be surprised." Aunt Dorothy responded, a knowing smile across her face. She wisely dropped the subject, knowing Lizzie would just dig her stubborn heels in deeper. Besides she had a feeling Lizzie would discover soon enough how helpful Bennett might be.

After supper Aunt Dorothy gave Mr. Lee a call asking him to come to church with them on Sunday followed by Sunday dinner at their home. Mr. Lee quickly agreed—he had never turned a meal down at the Long house. Aunt Dorothy was well known by many in the community to set a gracious table that left all who partook more than satisfied.

Lizzie spent a long time on the porch contemplating her future. On the beach she had focused too much on the past and her despair over the woulda, shoulda, coulda's. After talking about her ideas to move forward with Aunt Dorothy she felt a shift in her thinking and in her outlook. It was scary to think about starting over, but at the same time it was exhilarating and she felt her energy level returning. The pity party had come to a close.

That night Lizzie slept peaceful and deep. Her dreams were a whirl of sticking it to Mark, looking at large bank balances and basking in the glow of being near Bennett. She woke as the sun was peeking over the horizon. She stretched and smiled widely, for the first time in weeks she had a sense of direction. She jumped out of bed with so much energy the dogs leapt to get out of the way. Bennett danced across her mind and she did not feel the need to push the thought aside. She wanted to prove to him she had changed. When she did look into Bennett's eyes again she wanted to be sure she would not see any pity there.

Chapter Five

Lizzie watched as Bennett, his parents and his sister Amy with her husband and kids settled into the pew across the main aisle and two rows up from where Aunt Dorothy and Lizzie sat. One of Amy's kids, her youngest and only girl, climbed into Bennett's lap and snuggled into the crook of his arm. She was wearing a smocked seersucker pink and white sundress with ribbons tied at the shoulders. Bennett bent his head down and was saying something to her and although Lizzie could not hear what it was, she could tell by the smile on the little girl's face it was a tender moment between the uncle and his niece. Lizzie felt a tug at her heart. Bennett had always been so good with kids, it reminded her of Uncle George. She reached out and patted Aunt Dorothy's hand at the thought. Aunt Dorothy must miss Uncle George so much.

Mr. Lee joined them in the pew just as the organ and choir launched into the opening hymn. Lizzie dutifully followed the service, reciting the congregation's lines from the prayer book, singing the hymns and bowing her head for prayers. But, she found herself sneaking peeks at Bennett throughout and often observed him keeping a nephew on task or soothing his niece who had remained perched in his lap.

Amy had four children—three boys and one girl— and apparently did not utilize the church nursery. But—to her credit and that of the extended family, the children were not disruptive. No doubt Mrs. McGantry would have given them a scowl of disapproval if they had been. She had already turned around from her front row seat to scowl at Lizzie and Aunt Dorothy when she saw that Mr. Lee was sitting next to Aunt Dorothy in the pew. Not that it was unusual; Mr. Lee was actually a member of the Baptist church a few blocks away, but over the years he had joined Dorothy and George on occasion for church, particularly if they had plans together for Sunday brunch.

Mr. Lee was a confirmed bachelor and often spent time with the Longs. During the sermon Lizzie felt her cheeks burning. It seemed the theme of the week for Lizzie was now the theme for the congregation. Reverend Truett was preaching on the human failing of shallowly judging thy neighbor on outward appearances, not the content of their soul and who were they to judge that which was only for God to deem worthy or unworthy. Lizzie felt herself shrinking down into the pew, feeling like a spotlight was shining down from heaven on her head. In her line of sight she saw Mrs. McGantry straighten her shoulders, oblivious of the fact she was just as guilty as her fellow parishioners. Evidently she saw her judgments as divinely issued.

After the service they moved to the parish hall for coffee and greetings. Reverend Truett gave Dorothy a warm hug and heartily shook Mr. Lee's hand commenting, "We will convert you to Episcopalian yet, Tommy!"

Mr. Lee chuckled and replied, "Not until my mama won't roll over in her grave, but excellent sermon as always."

Once in the hall Mr. Lee went to fetch coffee for himself and the ladies and Lizzie scanned the room. The black and white tile floor and the warm wood wainscot-paneled room never seemed to change. Of course every Sunday it was the meet and greet space, but she had years of memories, vacation bible school, youth group dances, parish pancake suppers , so many events in her life. Aunt Dorothy excused herself to visit with the organist.

Mrs. Wilson, Bennett's mother, approached and embraced Lizzie. "I am so glad you are sticking around. Your Aunt Dorothy will be mighty glad for the company," she said. Lizzie smiled at her and replied. "I think I am back permanently. I can't believe how much I have missed by being away. I am amazed by Amy's family."

"Me too, sugar, I'm amazed to be a memaw four times over! It has been a joy in my life."

The two women looked over at the two youngest of Amy's brood who were giving Mrs. McGantry their rapt attention as she was telling them some kind of story. Their eyes were as big as saucers. Mrs. McGantry had a soft grandmotherly look about her as she interacted with the youngsters.

"Bless her heart," Mrs. Wilson sighed. "Marie would have been a wonderful grandmother. How sad that she didn't get the chance."

Lizzie witnessed a side to Mrs. McGantry she had never seen before.

"I'm sure your Aunt Dorothy will make a wonderful grandmother to your children too, Lizzie," Mrs. Wilson said. "Dorothy told me about your split from your husband. I am truly sorry, but don't give up on love. You would make a fine wife and mother with the right person," she added.

"Thank you. You have always been so kind to me, even when I was not so kind to Bennett," Lizzie replied.

"Oh, I was disappointed when you and Bennett broke up. I had gotten used to the idea you would be my daughter-in-law, but I also understood y'all were so young. Each of you needed to get out in the world and learn a bit more about yourselves. Now that you both have done that, I have to admit I'm rooting for a reunion between you two."

Lizzie blushed and stammered. "I ... I ... would be blessed to have a mother-in-law like you. I just don't think I can even consider romance, at least not until my divorce is final."

"Well, I better see how many cookies Mr. Wilson has snuck off the children's table. Lizzie, my door is always open to you if you want to talk or just come and visit," Mrs. Wilson said as she hugged Lizzie once more.

Lizzie hugged her back. "I would love to spend some time with you and tell you about my new project. I will come by soon," Lizzie said.

As Mrs. Wilson moved away, Lizzie looked around the hall. Her eyes landed on Bennett and she felt her face getting hot as she realized he was looking at her. Did he know she had been watching him in the church? Bennett smiled at her and she found herself smiling back despite the fact her brain was screaming, "*Don't encourage him!*"

Bennett turned away as two of his nephews went tearing by and almost knocked their grandmother off her feet. Lizzie looked down as she felt an unexpected breeze ruffle the bottom of her skirt and found herself looking into the blue-green eyes of a small boy with wavy black hair. He was looking up at her grinning, wait not at her face, but up her skirt!

Like his brothers, he was decked out in seersucker shorts, a white polo shirt and Dockers.

"Jeremy!" His mother scolded and quickly stood him up on his feet. "Apologize to Miss Long!"

"Sorry" Jeremy said with a wicked grin on his face that really said he was not.

"Sorry what?" his mom prompted.

"Sorry, ma'am," he obediently replied and quickly scampered away to join his siblings at the cookie table.

"I am so sorry," Amy said, looking embarrassed. "Don't be silly, it's a case of nephew like uncle the way I see it," Lizzie replied. In her mind's eye she was remembering a young boy of eight doing that same body slide on this floor to her eight year old self.

"He does look an awful lot like my brother and acts like him too," Amy said with a mock look of dismay but her smiling eyes said she was really pleased her son was like her brother. They were very close.

Lizzie could not disagree; she thought of an imaginary child with Mark's character and again felt relief she had not had a child with that man.

"Listen Amy, sorry I haven't contacted you since I have been back. The last five weeks have been a whirlwind."

"I totally get it, but I would love to have you over to the house and catch up."

"I would love that!" Lizzie exclaimed. She and Amy had managed to keep a friendship despite her split with Bennett a decade ago. They were not the kind of friends who shared all their secrets, but having known each other all their lives and at one time believing they would be sisters' in-law, they had never been able to sever ties.

"Hey, babe, we need to get lunch into the munchkins or we are going to have a cookie mutiny on our hands," Amy's husband Scott said, as he leaned in and gave Lizzie a peck on the cheek. "Nice to have you back around Lizzie, we'll have to get you over and we'll fire up the grill," he said. "I was just saying we needed to get her over to the house," Amy chimed in. "How about next Friday, around six?"

"Sounds good, what can I bring?" Lizzie asked. "Your pimento cheese spread," they said in unison and without skipping a beat.

"Well then, pimento cheese spread it is," and Lizzie smiled with self-satisfaction. It was gratifying how quickly they had answered. They obviously remembered her cooking fondly. She may have her first two customers, after Aunt Dorothy and Mr. Lee of course. If things went well with Mr. Lee over lunch, she could share her business idea with Amy and Scott on Friday.

"See you then," they chorused to each other and Lizzie watched the Wilson and Hutchins' clan exit out into the late June haze. *What a great family,* Lizzie thought wistfully.

She turned to see Aunt Dorothy and Mr. Lee engaged in conversation with Mrs. McGantry. Watching the expressions on their faces, she could tell Mrs. McGantry was expressing disapproval over something. Then she was startled to see Mrs. McGantry blush and giggle like a teenager in response to something Mr. Lee said to her. She had always thought of Mrs. McGantry as a stuffy, judgmental busybody, but maybe like so many others she had misjudged her.

Reverend Truett's sermon reverberated as she chided herself for judging others and vowed to improve. She walked over to collect Aunt Dorothy and Mr. Lee. It was time to get them back to the house and reveal the plans she had shared with Aunt Dorothy to Mr. Lee. She would need his help to get things started.

"Mrs. McGantry, that shade of pink looks lovely on you," she said as she approached the threesome.

"Why, how kind of you to say," Mrs. McGantry twittered back, a look of pleasure at the compliment lighting up her face. "Well, I must get home, glad to see you are going to be sticking around Lizzie. This is truly where you belong," Mrs. McGantry commented as she turned to exit as many of the parishioners had begun to thin out.

"Well, ladies, I am looking forward to hearing what Lizzie has planned, but truth be told I am practically salivating at the thought of Sunday lunch in your gracious home," Mr. Lee declared. Lizzie, with a flourish of her hand, led the way and they headed back to the house.

At the house Mr. Lee plopped his linen napkin down on the shiny surface of the dining room table. Aunt Dorothy's formal dining room was traditional with dark woods and silver julep cups sparkling on the sideboard. Many of the furnishings had been in the Long family for generations. The silver had a warm patina and was engraved with an S. It had belonged to Aunt Dorothy's mother, Lizzie's grandmother, and they used it lovingly. The S stood for Sawyer, which would have been Lizzie's maiden name had she not been formally adopted by Aunt Dorothy and Uncle George, a decision she had never regretted. The room was also warm and inviting with well-cushioned seats, deep blue walls and a plush oriental rug underfoot. Some of the paintings that hung in ornate frames had been painted by Lizzie's mother, who had been a budding professional artist at the time of her death. It was easy to linger over a meal in this room.

"That was one of the best tomato pies you have ever made, Dorothy," Mr. Lee commented as Lizzie whisked away his plate and headed to the kitchen to serve up the blackberry cobbler and whipped cream sitting in wait.

Dorothy smiled, "Well, Tommy, I can't take credit for anything sat before you today, as Lizzie was in charge of the kitchen."

"Really, very impressive Lizzie," he called out, "and a credit to your teaching skills, Dorothy," he added.

"Why thank you, Mr. Lee," Lizzie replied as she sat before him the delectable dish of cobbler and cream.

"There is a reason for this feast and not just our genuine affection for you," Aunt Dorothy said as she watched Tommy take his first bite and involuntarily sigh with pleasure as the tart berries, sugary crust and cooling cream danced across his tongue. "We, I mean Lizzie, needs your help," Dorothy continued.

"Well, all you have to do is ask," he said. "Plying me with food is not necessary, but greatly appreciated," he replied, winking at Lizzie.

"Well, food is kind of the point," Lizzie said. "I want to use some of my windfall to start a business. A shop/tea room type of place, I want to serve breakfast/ brunch/lunch type food, coffee, tea ... and also sell food products, take-out tomato pies and other things ... what do you think?" she timidly asked.

"I think you have a daily lunch customer sitting right here," he smiled. "We need to make sure you are in walking distance from my office," he laughed.

"That's what we need you for," Dorothy chimed in. "We need to get her a place, a business plan, permits etc."

"I would be glad to help. One of my partners, Mr. Smith, is an expert in the permit process, so between the two of us we can definitely get you on your feet. Come by my office tomorrow around noon. On my lunch break I want to take you to see what I think might be a perfect location. I happen to work often with the owner and I think he will offer you a fair deal. You are also fortunate to be able to fund this venture without the need for a loan, which will also make this process easier."

Lizzie flung her arms around Mr. Lee. "Thank you so much!"

"Lizzie, I'm not doing this because I love you like family. You are seriously a talented cook and I know you have some background knowledge in business from your past work experience. I really believe you can make a success from this venture," Mr. Lee exhorted.

Lizzie, humbled by the vote of confidence, blushed and in a low voice replied, "That means more to me than you can possibly know."

Lizzie spent the afternoon, writing out her ideas in a notebook. *What do I want my business to look like? How will my customers experience my food?* She did not want to be strictly a restaurant, she also wanted to provide gift baskets and prepared casseroles for folks to take home and feed their families with the love that can only come from homemade. With so many households these days having both parents working, it would be a nice alternative to frozen entrees or fast food take-out. She wanted to reflect the bounty of the sea and the local farms. She wanted her customers to feel like they were visiting a friend, but what to call it?

She definitely had some business skills; she understood marketing and could read contracts and ledgers with confidence. What she didn't know was sources for all the things she would need. She wasn't even sure what she needed. This time as her mind began to whirl with questions she didn't feel despair, instead she felt energized. Her confidence felt a boost.

By early evening she had sketched out a business plan and made a list of all she needed to research to flesh it out. She could begin to see what her future could be and that made it easier to leave her past and the questions about it behind. It was so nice to concentrate on something positive for a change. She was blessed with people in her life who would help her along the way.

What would Mark say when he found out about her money? It really did not matter, Mr. Lee had made sure that Lizzie and her money were legally protected from him ever getting his hands on it. Still, she took some satisfaction imagining the expression on his face if he ever found out. If only the divorce could happen faster. Now that she was moving on with her life, she wanted that to apply to all areas. Luckily with all she had to keep her busy and the fact they were living on opposite ends of the state, she hoped she would not dwell on it much.

She stepped out on the back porch to take the dogs out before bed and gasped. The full moon hovered over the harbor, casting a magical trail of light across the water that seemed to reach right to their dock. It surprised her that even after growing up here, the beauty of the lowcountry could still catch her breath. The sparkle of the moonlight dancing on the harbor was mesmerizing. She sat on the back steps and Lucky and Ella came and sat vigil at her feet. The soft breeze fluttered the Spanish moss and caressed her face. She sat for a long time captivated by the view before sleep beckoned her to climb the stairs.

Chapter Six

Lizzie sat in Mr. Lee's waiting area a few minutes before noon. She could hardly contain her excitement. She knew she was fortunate to have capital to start her business with, but she was also blessed to have the guidance and connections Mr. Lee and his associates would avail her. She wrote questions down in her notebook as they came to her and when the clock struck twelve, Mr. Lee, as punctual as ever, strode out from his office, dapper in his seersucker suit, the summer uniform for lowcountry attorneys.

"Hello Lizzie, ready to see your new home away from home?"

"Of course and here," she said, handing Mr. Lee a brown bag.

"What's this?" he asked.

"A fresh egg salad sandwich and a homemade moon pie. It's the least I can do as you are taking up your lunch time to help me."

"Mmmm ... mmmm, I am going to leave that here in the icebox and enjoy it when I come back to tackle the mound of paperwork waiting for me on my desk."

After stowing the lunch Mr. Lee and Lizzie headed out into the sultry summer air. It was a short walk to the corner of Coleman Boulevard, and just a block down they stopped in front of a rectangular, one story cinder-block building that had for years been a bike shop and in the recent past had been a Mexican restaurant. The tenants at that time had added a nice wide screened porch on the front with a tin roof. Some straw sombreros still decorated the walls of the porch.

"I remember this place," Lizzie exclaimed. "This would be a great location. Will the landlord allow for alterations to the property?"

"As a matter of fact, yes, and they are open to a lease with option to buy the property after two years if you so choose," answered Mr. Lee. "I thought of this place because it already has a kitchen, and I think it will require minimal remodeling to get to the vision you shared with me. I have the key, let's go in and take a gander," he continued.

The inside was a little dusty and there was a long bar that definitely needed to be removed, but Lizzie could envision what it could look like and allowed herself to get excited about the possibilities. Despite the porch that ran the length of the front of the building, the space seemed to have good natural light. The floor was concrete and could be painted and have coats of polyurethane applied for durability. They stepped on to the porch and she loved the effect the tin roof had on the space.

"What is the monthly rent on this place?" she asked.

"It has been running two-thousand a month, but I have it on good authority that the landlord is willing to rent for sixteen-hundred as it has been sitting vacant for a while."

"And who owns it?" Lizzie continued to probe. "An investment company called B.E.W. Enterprise," he answered.

"So how do we make this happen?" Lizzie continued. "We will go back to the office and start the paperwork. You will need to give me a list of the alterations to the property you would like to have happen as soon as possible, and if approved the landlord will send a work crew over to make it happen. You will be responsible for tables, chairs, shelving etc. and you may also pick the colors of paint you would like to use."

"Good, I would like to make it feel like a coastal cottage in here." Lizzie's eyes wandered over the walls.

"We should also carefully look over the kitchen equipment that is here and see if it meets your needs." Mr. Lee smiled broadly. "I can't wait until I can make this my regular lunch place."

The two carefully looked over the kitchen and Lizzie took lots of notes and made a few sketches on a note pad. The kitchen was more than adequately equipped even having a large commercial freezer and a walk-in cooler. The handle was a little loose on the cooler but otherwise it was in great condition like the other equipment. That certainly would make getting up and running a lot easier. Off the kitchen there was a walk-in storage closet, a large walk-in pantry, a small office and a bathroom. The backdoor led out to a small parking lot.

They headed back to the office and signed the required paperwork, and Lizzie set up an appointment with Mr. Smith to get the permit process and business license started.

She gave Mr. Lee a big hug and a kiss on the cheek. "Thank you, thank you!" she exclaimed.

"It was my pleasure Lizzie. You just keep making me your delicious food and I will do just about anything for you ... at least within the parameters of the law," he said as he winked at her.

"Yes, sir!" Lizzie responded. "See you soon," she added as she almost skipped out the door.

Lizzie left that afternoon with her feet floating off the ground. Aunt Dorothy listened enthusiastically as Lizzie described the space and shared her vision of what it could become. They discussed colors and counter top options and Lizzie showed her the refrigerated cases she needed to purchase on her laptop. Then the two worked side by side to prepare their supper.

~

After supper Lizzie felt herself consumed by nervous energy so she dusted off her old beach cruiser from the garage and took it for a spin. She thought she had been riding aimlessly but realized she had been closing in on the block where the Wilson's lived. As she approached the house she saw Mr. and Mrs. Wilson enjoying the early evening out on their front porch, and they both waved as they saw her. Lizzie dismounted from her bike and climbed the steps, giving them both a hug.

"Can I offer you some lemonade, or something a little stronger?" asked Mr. Wilson.

"Lemonade would be lovely," she answered.

He went in to fetch a glass for her and Mrs. Wilson informed her, "You just missed Bennett. He stopped by to help his father re-hang the screened door on the back porch."

Lizzie smiled, "He helps out a lot at my house as well," she said, recalling her embarrassment at finding him at her window.

"Oh, yes, he had a special relationship with your Uncle George. He credits your Uncle George with teaching him so many skills. He has taken his passing really hard," Mrs. Wilson explained.

"Here is some of my wife's fresh squeezed lemonade," said Mr. Wilson as he re-emerged onto the porch.

"Thank you, sir," Lizzie said as she gratefully accepted the glass.

"So, my bride tells me you plan to return home for good, we will be blessed for it. What are you going to do to keep yourself out of trouble young lady?" Mr. Wilson asked. Lizzie, flattered by his enthusiasm at her return, eagerly shared with them her plans to open her own business and how Mr. Lee had found her the perfect location.

"B.E.W. Enterprises, huh? I hear that is a first rate organization, don't think you can go wrong there," Mr. Wilson commented.

"That is good to hear," Lizzie said.

After another glass of lemonade, hearing about Mr. Wilson's plan to retire in the next year and Mrs. Wilson's new passion for knitting, she bade them goodnight and pedaled home. She was elated by the genuine affection the Wilsons still had for her and her for them.

Back at the house she contemplated the gathering at Amy's house. She fervently hoped her reconnection to her peers would be as smooth as with the Wilsons.

~

The next few days passed in a whirlwind of researching sources for her needs and making the list of the alterations she wished to make to the space. By Thursday afternoon she was confident in her plans and submitted the requests via Mr. Lee.

On Friday morning she turned her attention to her plans to go over to Amy's for the cookout and even though she was keen to rekindle her local friendships she was also dreading the inevitable questions that would come about what had happened with Mark. She also saw the social gathering as a distraction from the immersion, let's admit, obsession she felt about her new venture. She found it hard to pry her attention away from the business. Aunt Dorothy was pleased Lizzie was going to Amy's. She wanted her to socialize, and she was concerned Lizzie was using the business as an excuse to avoid human interaction. Particularly, interaction with those of the opposite gender.

She was standing in the kitchen working on the butcher block counter next to the sink so she could gaze out at the waving marsh grasses as she worked. The butcher block had a warm and worn patina from years of use. Aunt Dorothy oiled it regularly and while the kitchen was not fancy or "upgraded" like the remodels many of the neighbors had completed, it was the true heart of this home. Lizzie remembered standing on a chair to reach this same counter so she could watch and assist Aunt Dorothy in all kinds of tasks. In her teen years the kitchen was often the place they would talk over things as they would sit companionably shelling butter beans, peeling shrimp or shucking corn.

It was a large space and had changed very little over the years. The one indulgence, a state of the art range with six burners and two large oven chambers, had been added when the previous range finally quit three years ago. Uncle George had even installed an industrial strength vent hood to support the BTU's. Lizzie had been envious, and was really enjoying using it since she had moved back home. Today's task was to make the requested pimento cheese spread for the cookout. Which did not involve using the range but considering the unrelenting summer heat that was fine with her. *This is definitely one item I will need to serve and have available for takeout orders.*

Aunt Dorothy came in and sat down at the long pine table in the center of the room. "Well, this is like old times. I am so glad you are here, child."

"I am glad to be here," answered Lizzie. The kitchen table had been witness to many heart to hearts over the years. Lizzie felt the love in this room and with this woman who took her in and raised her.

Lizzie proceeded to tell Aunt Dorothy about the final plans she had submitted to the landlord, and when Lizzie finished she asked Aunt Dorothy for her thoughts.

"It sounds well thought out," she replied.

"Well, I have envisioned this place in my mind for the better part of the last decade," Lizzie said.

"What are you going to call the place?" Aunt Dorothy asked. "I was thinking Dorothy's," Lizzie answered turning to see the reaction on Aunt Dorothy's face.

With a grateful smile Aunt Dorothy replied, "While I am flattered and so appreciate the sentiment behind the gesture, this is your dream child, not mine, I think you should consider some other options."

"Well, I do have a few other ideas, East Cooper Eatery, East Cooper Café, Lizzie's, but nothing seems to fit just right," Lizzie answered.

"Give yourself some time; the right name will come to you. I also have a dream, a plan if you will, and I think it is time I let you in on it," Aunt Dorothy continued.

Lizzie, having just put the bowl of her pimento cheese spread in the fridge, wiped her hands on a towel and came to join Dorothy at the table.

"What's going on?" she asked curious, but not surprised. Aunt Dorothy was not one to wallow in grief or see her new status as widow as restrictive in any way.

"I had planned to ask Tommy over for dinner next week so he could be here for support, but now that I see that you are doing better, I can't see any reason we need him here to help me fill you in," she started.

"Okay, now you are making me nervous," Lizzie said, as she reached across the table to take Aunt Dorothy's hand in hers.

"Well, as you know Maggie lost her husband three years ago and now that Uncle George is gone, the two of us are both footloose and fancy free as the saying goes. Back when we were in college we both wanted to study abroad, or at least travel, but Maggie got engaged and shortly after that I did too. Well, that put a stop to our plans. So now we have time and we also both have more than enough funds to take an extended and by that, I mean a many months-long trip that will take us all over the globe to the many places we have always wanted to experience. What do you think?"

Lizzie felt the ground fall out from under her and she blurted out her first reaction. "You're leaving me?"

"Not leaving you, child, following my own path and giving you the space to find yours, I of course want you to stay here in the house and look after things. Besides you will be so busy launching your new business, you won't even miss me."

"Of course I'll miss you!" Lizzie exclaimed.

Aunt Dorothy reached over and cupped Lizzie's chin in her hand, turning her face so she could peer directly into her eyes. "Elizabeth Caroline Long, you can stand on your own two feet! I have full faith in you, besides I won't leave until September fifteenth so I will be here for your grand opening in August."

Lizzie felt the ground return underneath her and she smiled and with genuine gladness replied, "I guess there is not much more to say except bon voyage, although I want to hear all about your itinerary. Plus we need to have a communication plan in place. Have you ever Skyped?" Lizzie asked.

"No, child, but I am sure you can teach me. I'm not afraid to learn new things," Aunt Dorothy answered.

They went out onto the porch with some iced tea and Aunt Dorothy shared her and Maggie's plan to travel all over Europe. They would take in England, Ireland, Scotland, France, Spain, Belgium, the Netherlands, Germany, Switzerland, Italy and Greece. There was a short stop in Egypt to see the Pyramids, an exotic jaunt through Asia, with the Great Wall of China being one of the highlights. They had even planned a few weeks exploring New Zealand and Australia. It was ambitious but the ladies were giving themselves September to April for their adventures. The travel agency had pre-booked flights, trains, ground transport, accommodations and even tickets for some of the must- sees along their way. In Egypt they would even have a private guide, which had become almost essential for foreign tourists to maintain their safety.

Lizzie could not help but marvel at the gumption these two ladies in their seventies had. She was also a little jealous of what they would experience, but she knew her time for such a trip would come. She evidently would have the funds, what she lacked was the ideal companion—a trip like that was meant to be shared. That was why going to Amy and Scott's house was so important. She needed to reconnect with her peers and rebuild her friendships.

Later that afternoon the phone rang as Lizzie was contemplating what to wear for the first social outing she had attended since her return. It was Mr. Lee with good news, the landlord had approved the alterations and she could meet the work crew at the site on Monday morning. She would take possession of her own set of keys and the crew would begin the demolition. Everything was falling into place. *Almost too easily*, she mused at least with the business, and that made her nervous that something was bound to go wrong. She pushed that thought aside. After all the new Lizzie vowed to be positive and true to herself. *Now, what to wear?* The green halter-neck sundress that emphasized her shoulders or the pink and white Lily Pulitzer dress with the sleeves but the shorter hemline that showed off her legs?

Chapter Seven

Lizzie made one last check in the mirror before heading downstairs to say goodnight to Aunt Dorothy and head out for Amy and Scott's house. She had settled on the emerald green sundress, liking the effect it had in bringing out the green in her hazel eyes. Her hair she had hot rolled for maximum body and then brought it up in back into a loose up-do to give her neck some relief in the heat. She was feeling very self-conscious about the dent in her finger where her wedding ring used to be, so after rifling through her jewelry box she had found an emerald cocktail ring that had once belonged to her mother.

Aunt Dorothy had done an exceptional job keeping the memory of Lizzie's parents alive. She had presented her with various pieces of her mother's jewelry, always with a story of when and where her mother had worn it over the course of her upbringing. When she wore one of the pieces, she felt connected to her mother. She wondered sometimes what her mother would think about how she had turned out. She knew how blessed she was to have Aunt Dorothy and had always felt loved and secure. But because she had been so young when her mother had died, she had created an image of her that no one could live up to in real life.

She imagined that had her mother lived, she would not have made the mistake of falling for Mark in the first place. She slipped on the ring and immediately felt like she had gained a talisman to boost her confidence. The ring went well with the dress and she selected a simple gold necklace with a single emerald pendant, a graduation gift from Aunt Dorothy and Uncle George, and some simple gold dangling earrings to complete the look. Lizzie debated between heels and flats and her practical side won out. She slid on her gold braided sandals.

She gave Aunt Dorothy a quick peck on the cheek and retrieved the pimento cheese spread from the fridge and a basket of crackers to go with it. She gave Lucky and Ella a treat and headed out the door. It was a short drive to Scott and Amy's; although both of them had grown up in the Old Village, they had bought a house in a golf course development called Snee Farm. Their house was in a cul-de-sac, perfect for their four kids and only blocks from the club house and pool.

Lizzie was a little surprised to see how many cars seemed to be there and when she approached the door she could hear the promised small gathering was much larger than anticipated. Although as the door opened and Bennett welcomed her in, she was grateful for the crowd.

Amy came towards her. "Lizzie, so glad you could make it! This party has taken on a life of its own! We kept running into people all week and the guest list kept getting bigger and bigger," Amy offered, almost apologetically in her explanation. She seemed to sense Lizzie's unease.

"Sounds like it's going to be fun," Lizzie replied, as if trying to convince herself. Bennett had disappeared as fast as he had appeared and Lizzie found herself looking around for him. She spied him just as he stepped out onto the back porch. "Um ... here is the pimento cheese spread as requested."

"Great! Let's put that out on the dining room table. I'm keeping the food in there so we don't have to worry about bugs or heat," Amy replied. "You won't believe who I ran into at the farmer's market this week; your one and only best bud, M.A.! She and Jim are in town through the weekend and they are coming tonight, just as soon as they drop off the girl's at Jim's parent's house. M.A. says they have spent the past couple of days just chauffeuring the kids between her parent's house and his parent's house for equitable visitation. The grandparents apparently are very jealous of each other," Amy continued.

"I'm not surprised," Lizzie said. "Their Christmas card this year in those smocked dresses was too cute. I can't wait to catch up with her."

Amy went off to attend to some of the other guests and Lizzie went in search of the wine. She thought about her friendship with M.A., Mary Ann to the majority of the world. They had been friends for as long as she could remember. She had been M.A.'s maid of honor and M.A. had been her matron of honor. M.A. had married her high school sweetheart Jim and the two couples, M.A. and Jim and she and Bennett, had been tight. When Lizzie and Bennett had broken up it had been hardest on M.A. and Jim. M.A. had been supportive of her relationship with Mark, but Mark had been critical of her friendship with M.A. and when they had left to go to Columbia for Mark's law school, he had discouraged close contact between the friends. Despite his efforts, they had done a good job staying in touch at first. Then Jim, a Citadel engineering grad, had gotten a job offer with a firm in Richmond, Virginia and with M.A., who had earned her nursing degree from the Medical University, had pulled up their roots and relocated. In the past six years they had doubled their family with two beautiful girls, Elizabeth (Lizzie's namesake and god child) and Rebecca. So over time the friends had been caught up in their separate lives, talking on the phone occasionally and exchanging Christmas cards. So it came as no surprise to Lizzie that she had been unaware the Huttos were in town for a family visit, or that M.A. was unaware she was still here after the funeral or the circumstances that brought her home to stay.

Lizzie took a moment to scan the crowd. She recognized a lot of faces and a few new ones. People smiled at her and she smiled back. At first she chose to chat with the new folks who would know nothing of her, then slowly made the rounds to old acquaintances as she gained confidence. All her old pals graciously offered condolences about Uncle George and inquired after Aunt Dorothy. All were careful to avoid mentioning Mark or inquiring to his whereabouts, which told her the community grapevine was alive and well.

She appreciated the fact she did not need to explain and enjoyed that a few souls dared to make a brief comment to the effect of good riddance, you deserve so much better, all indicating they believed her to be in the right and Mark in the wrong. She needed to feel accepted and not judged and her friends were accommodating that in spades. It was also enjoyable to learn how the past few years had passed for these acquaintances and she regretted she had not done a better job keeping in touch.

By the time she had made the rounds she felt like she had slipped into a comfortable pair of pajamas. Being social with this crowd was so different from the crowd Mark had insisted they socialize with. Here she was accepted as herself and she genuinely liked the people, *her people,* around her. Conspicuously absent from each little group she chatted with was Bennett. He always seemed to be moving onto the next group as she would approach. *Was he avoiding her?* Part of her wanted to share the news about the business with him, but she was a little afraid. What if he thought it was a lame idea? She did mention to a few folks that she was in the process of launching a new business, careful not to reveal too much. She received encouraging feedback that she had a winning concept.

"Lizzie!!!" she turned to see M.A. leaping towards her and the two embraced. Immediately she felt a piece of her soul warm, her friendship with M.A. had been greatly missed. Now she had a chance to rekindle that connection. "Let's grab some wine and find a spot we can talk. I know just the place!" M.A. took charge, grabbing a bottle in one hand and two glasses in the other while simultaneously hustling Lizzie into the backyard and over to two Adirondack style chairs tucked in the corner. Amy had thoughtfully set up citronella torches thinking guests might like to sit and visit.

"Now before you say anything, I didn't know you were here, until I ran into Amy at the farmer's market. I heard about Uncle George of course," M.A. began and Lizzie interrupted.

"Aunt Dorothy loved the hydrangea bush you sent and had me plant it in the garden immediately."

"I'm so glad, I'm just sorry I couldn't be here," M. A. continued. "The girls were still in school; Virginia had a crazy amount of snow days this year. And before you try and find a way to tell me about Mark, I already know."

"Let me guess, Amy again?" Lizzie stated more than asked.

"Actually it was my littlest sister, Rachael. Can you believe she is all grown up and working as a paralegal for Mr. Lee? Anyway, she handled some paperwork and although she realizes she should not talk about client's business, she felt she had to make an exception in this case because she was worried about you. So ... at first I didn't believe her and I sent a card to your address in Greenville and it came back to me, return to sender forwarding address unknown."

Lizzie thought to herself while M.A. talked on, *I can't believe Mark didn't even have the decency to forward my mail!*

I need to see what Mr. Lee can do about that! I wonder what else I might have missed.

"Then we were coming here this week so I knew I could find out what was going on from Aunt Dorothy, but before I could check in I ran into Amy, and she said you would be here tonight. The tug of war between my parent's and Jim's, well frankly it is wearing me out, we need our own turf in this town, which brings me to the best news of all. Jim interviewed with a local firm yesterday and it looks really promising. If it all works out we will be moving back here too!"

M.A. paused to take a sip of her wine and Lizzie chimed in, "I see we are starting in right where we left off, you talking a mile a minute and me waiting for you to drink so I can get a word in edgewise."

The two friends giggled and looked at each other. That was how you knew if a friendship was lifelong, when regardless of time or place that came between, once reunited there was a natural continuation of what had always been and the time past was but a blink.

M.A. sat back against the chair and let out a deep breath, "I'm going to show you my grown up self. I will sit and sip and you will talk my ear off, starting with how you came to your senses and what are your plans now and why despite my scintillating company I keep catching you spying glimpses of Bennett and tracking his movements."

Lizzie began to protest, but M.A. held up her hand, "Talk, woman, and don't leave out any details. Let's see how accurate the grapevine is these days."

So Lizzie sat back as well and spilled her soul; what had happened with Mark, her initial confusion and lack of direction and the soul searching and truth facing she had been working through. She told her how she had developed a plan and had even made concrete moves to put that plan into action, at least in the area of her professional life. She admitted she was still floundering when it came to her heart and shared her wish to find a good man.

Although she left out the encounters she had with Bennett, she did not want M.A. jumping on the "reunite with Bennett" bandwagon. M.A. grimaced and tsked while she told the tale of Mark and how their marriage had crumbled. She grinned and nodded as Lizzie shared her plans for a new business and Aunt Dorothy's plans to take a world tour.

"I remember in high school, when you wanted to earn money to get a new surf board and you sold boxes of biscuits door to door around the neighborhood. I do hope you are going to offer those in your café. What are you going to call it anyway?" M.A. asked.

"I'm not sure, but I'm getting a brainstorm here ... what do you think of ... of The Biscuit Box?" Lizzie looked at M.A's face for her reaction.

"I think that sounds like a place I'd like to eat," M.A. laughed. "So now that I have sparked your brain on that issue, let's see what we can do about you and Bennett."

"Please M.A. don't start, that relationship ended a long time ago. Besides Bennett seems to be directionless as ever, I can't even figure out what he does for a living," Lizzie replied.

"You mean you don't know?" started M.A.

"Know what?" Lizzie asked.

Before M.A. could answer, though, M.A's husband joined them.

"I hate to break up the reunion, but mom just called. Elizabeth has been throwing up for the past hour and while Grandma knows what to do, the patient only wants her mama."

"Well, duty calls," M.A. said as she stood up and handed her empty glass to Jim. "We will continue this conversation very soon, my love. I'll call you."

"Okay, I hope Elizabeth is feeling better soon. Jim, you better drive. M.A. had the lion's share of that bottle," Lizzie said, and gave them both a quick hug. They slipped into the house to make their goodbyes to their hostess.

I wonder what M.A. knows about Bennett? Lizzie wondered, but before she could muse on it too long one of the other guests came over, gushing about her pimento cheese spread and wondering if Lizzie could share the recipe. Flattered, Lizzie wrote it out on a napkin and as she finished, Amy who had come up on the other side of Lizzie, said, "Be careful, you don't want to give all your trade secrets away."

"How did you know about my new business?" Lizzie asked.

"I happen to be the bookkeeper for B.E.W. Enterprises and the new lease agreement was brought to my attention. I will be noting all your rent payments in the ledger," she explained.

"Well, I promise to be consistent and pay on time," Lizzie assured her.

"I have no doubt about that. I can't wait until you are open. I think you will be an instant hit among the locals and will attract tourist dollars as well," Amy shared.

"Thank you for your enthusiastic support and thank you for putting this gathering together; it was just what I needed to reconnect," Lizzie said, giving Amy a hug. Amy hugged her back and whispered in her ear,

"It's good to have you back where you belong."

Lizzie enjoyed listening to the tales of friends and their adventures in parenting. After another glass of wine as the crowd began to thin, Lizzie felt emboldened enough to approach Bennett with the intention of confronting him. She wanted to know if he was avoiding her and if so why. She found him standing in the grass chatting with Scott. She walked up and Scott, sensing she was a woman on a mission, made a gracious and speedy exit, leaving the pair standing there.

"I'm just going to lay it out there, have you been avoiding me tonight?"

"Actually I have," Bennett responded, catching Lizzie off guard.

She had anticipated he would deny her accusation. "Why the hell would you do that?" She blurted out before the truth of his response had hit her.

As soon as she said it, she wished she could take it back. She did not really want him to answer, as much as she had protested the idea of rekindling their relationship, she did not think her ego could handle the knowledge that he had closed the door on the idea before it could even be explored.

"It's not what you think, I'm sure," Bennett answered with a hint of exasperation, or was that sarcasm?

Lizzie did not have confidence in her ability to read people these days, least of all people of the male variety.

"It's just that since you've been back, you have kinda told me six ways to Sunday, you really don't want me around," he continued.

Lizzie sputtered as she tried to come up with a plausible response. The truth was he had interpreted her correctly, but she didn't want him to know that.

As she backed away, she managed to mutter, "It's not that I don't want you around, it's just all I'm dealing ..."

"Lizzie, stop!" Bennett shouted interrupting her lame attempt to justify her behavior over the past month and a half. He was too late. Lizzie felt the ground fly out from beneath her as she fell backwards, landing in the kids' baby pool.

In her attempt to back away from Bennett she had inadvertently in true Lizzie style, made a less than gracious exit. Lizzie sat stunned, the water sloshing around her. Amy and Scott came running.

Scott helped her up, while Amy scolded him, "Didn't I tell you to empty that and put it away before the party? I knew something like this would happen. I'm so sorry, Lizzie!"

"Oh, no big deal, at least I didn't melt like the Wicked Witch of the West," Lizzie replied and found herself laughing at her own mortification, which instantly put the hosts and the remaining guests at ease.

Despite the warm air, Lizzie felt a chill as her wet dress clung to her and she made a lame attempt to wring it out. Bennett had found a towel and handed it to her. She wrapped up and took Amy up on an offer to borrow some dry clothes from her. After a plate of food to make sure she was sober enough to drive, with her wet clothes stowed in a plastic bag, she said her goodbyes assuring Amy and Scott, no harm, no foul.

Later as Lizzie drove home, Amy's words came back to her, *glad to have you back where you belong*. She smiled as she realized Amy and M.A. were again part of her life and they genuinely wanted her in their lives. She felt another piece of her life slide back into place.

Chapter Eight

Lizzie stood outside the location for The Biscuit Box in anticipation of getting started. The heat was already building despite the early hour. The Carolina blue sky had barely a cloud in sight and the sunlight was almost blinding as it bounced off the white exterior of the building. Lizzie was grateful that the small back parking lot was heavily shaded by a mature live oak tree, its Spanish moss barely stirring in the thick air. Hopefully the sea breeze would kick in later to bring some relief.

The Biscuit Box ... leave it to M.A. to be the inspiration for the perfect name. She had a knack for saying just the right thing to get Lizzie on track. So why didn't she listen to her about Mark? Thinking back she couldn't recall talking to her much about him until after they were engaged. M.A. had been so busy in nursing school and keeping up with Jim at the Citadel, and Mark had always tried to get her to be friends with his hand selected acquaintances. Plus just like Aunt Dorothy and Uncle George, she probably thought Lizzie knew what she was doing. Lizzie knew she wouldn't have listened to M.A.'s misgivings about Mark any more than anyone else's. The sound of a motor jarred her back to the present.

A work truck and van pulled into the parking lot, both bearing the logo for B.E.W. Enterprises, and a crew of seven men got out. Bennett was one of them. He wore a t-shirt and shorts, but he had work boots on his feet. He also had on a ball cap, something he had worn religiously as a teenager.

"Good morning Lizzie," he said as he handed her a large brown envelope with B.E.W. Enterprises' logo on it and a set of keys.

"My, my Bennett, you sure put your handyman skills to good use," Lizzie replied, taking the keys up to the door and unlocking it.

The men unloaded some equipment and Bennett pulled out the plans and asked Lizzie if these were indeed the plans she had submitted and when she gave the acknowledgement that they were, he said, "Alright men, let's get to tearing out that bar."

"I see you are elevated to foreman on this job," Lizzie said. Bennett just grinned and tipped his cap to her and jumped right into the demolition.

Lizzie headed to the kitchen and began a fresh inspection of her equipment, making a list of supplies she still needed to get. She also got down to the business of giving everything a serious scrubbing. Over the next several hours the crew worked out in the front and Lizzie worked in the back, although through the door Lizzie could see Bennett stepping out to take phone calls quite frequently and leaving the bulk of the work to the other men. By lunch time the space was cleared of debris and cleaned up, ready for paint. Lizzie looked around the kitchen, now gleaming and ready for use. Her arms ached but her soul soared.

The men left for lunch and Lizzie went down the street to get a sandwich at the deli and some iced tea. She walked despite the heat. It was not very far and she realized that on some days she would be able to ride her bike to work.

It gave her the feeling of living in a small town, despite the growth and sprawl that had come to Mount Pleasant in the past few decades. Another nice thing about the Coleman location was that folks heading out to Sullivan's Island would pass her way. At the deli she ordered a sub sandwich and then introduced herself to the shop owner.

"Hi, I'm Lizzie Long. I am getting ready to open shop in August where the old Mexican restaurant used to be."

"Nice to meet you Lizzie, I'm Jason Mills, welcome."

They chatted a bit about running a small business and he encouraged her to join the merchant's association and the Chamber of Commerce. Then he left her alone so she could eat her sub in peace.

On the way back she passed a fabric shop and decided she would stop in to see if she could find fabric for chair cushions and maybe some outdoor fabric to hang curtains on the screened porch. Which got her thinking she needed chairs to have seat cushions on. She needed to find out if Page's Thieves Market could hook her up with chairs and tables. She envisioned chairs that did not match and she wanted an assortment of wooden tables she could paint in the chalk paint that was all the rage on Pinterest.

Her list of what to do was getting longer and longer but she didn't feel overwhelmed, she felt exhilarated. She spent some time introducing herself to the staff at the fabric store, and they promised to stop in once she was open. With the expert help of a delightful sales associate who reminded her a little of Bennett's mom, she narrowed it down to some ocean-inspired fabric with whimsical star- fish and other sea creatures and a coordinating stripe that would go with the coastal cottage vibe she wanted in the space. There were so many beautiful fabrics it was hard to stay focused. *I wonder if Aunt Dorothy would do the sewing for me*, Lizzie thought.

She may have gained her cooking prowess from Aunt Dorothy, but she had not had the patience to learn the sewing, smocking and fine needlework Aunt Dorothy had tried to teach her. Now she regretted it a bit, but luckily there were still many around who excelled and enjoyed the sewing and the smocking. It was a little sad to think so many young southern women were like Lizzie, and were not appreciating the gift of instruction in the sewing arts from the older women in their families.

She headed back to The Biscuit Box and found the men painting but no Bennett in sight.

"That looks great guys!" Lizzie said as she entered, thinking to herself the blue color the paint company had named Beach House was the perfect choice for the main walls. "I see your esteemed foreman Mr. Wilson has ducked out on the work."

The men chuckled and then one of them said, "Mr. Wilson, he isn't the foreman, he is the CEO of B.E.W. Enterprises. He's our boss and your landlord. He's off at one of his other companies, the offshore fishing charter. He likes to personally take out a couple of the charters each week."

Lizzie was too stunned to reply but felt her face grow hotter and hotter. Bennett was her landlord! He owned multiple businesses? Then her brain settled on the fact that she was legally bound to Bennett by the lease for the next two years. *You can bet I'm going to exercise that option to buy when the terms are up*, she thought. She should have known!

B.E.W. Enterprises, B. E.W. stood for Bennett Edward Wilson. Why did it seem that the universe was conspiring to throw him in her face? She fumed and stewed. She called M.A. and ranted about her perceived predicament, but M.A. only pointed out that at least she had a hands-on landlord, and hadn't he given her a deal on the lease and gone along with all her requests for the remodel? M.A., the voice of reason, helped her calm down and realize this revelation was not the end of the world.

She hung up and although she was suspicious Aunt Dorothy and Mr. Lee had been well aware who owned the building she was leasing, she knew it really was an ideal set up and had she known who owned it beforehand she would not have even considered it. It also dawned on her Amy had known she was leasing from her brother, but she must have thought Lizzie knew who owned B.E.W. Enterprises.

The rest of the afternoon she was too busy to give it more thought as she made list after list of all the things she needed to accomplish and things she needed to purchase and track down. As the late afternoon sun became early evening she barely noticed and was startled when she heard Aunt Dorothy's voice saying, "Child, it's almost seven and you have been here since seven this morning. You don't have to do it all today."

Lizzie suddenly became aware of how tired her brain was and how much her stomach was growling. Aunt Dorothy looked around. "This color is you Lizzie. It's coastal but with an edge of sophistication, cool but warm if that makes sense," she said.

"I love it," Lizzie replied, pleased that her Aunt saw her in the space already.

"So, The Biscuit Box is off to a good start! Now let's go get you some dinner, child and then we can take Lucky and Ella for a nice walk down to Alhambra Hall." Aunt Dorothy directed Lizzie and she obediently gathered up her lap top, note pad and purse. She locked the door behind them and they headed back to the house.

~

Over a delicious dinner of seared scallops over a spinach and bacon salad along with some French rolls and creamy butter, Lizzie told Aunt Dorothy all about the revelation that Bennett was her landlord. Aunt Dorothy took a long sip of her iced tea before she offered Lizzie her thoughts on the situation.

"Well, that makes me feel good about the situation. We know his people. He sits in the same church we do and banks at the same bank, and I believe we go to the same dentist and doctor. The way I see it, he wouldn't be anything but fair and honorable in his dealings with you. Besides, it's not like he is your business partner, although being a successful small business owner, I am sure he could offer you all kinds of guidance as things come up." She smiled at Lizzie, a little too much like the Cheshire cat, but Lizzie didn't dare to call her out on it.

Lizzie then told her all about the progress made today and finding the fabric for the store.

"I would be happy to make the curtains for you child," Aunt Dorothy offered. "I think you might want to see if the seat fabric can be laminated to make it easy to wipe off."

"I hadn't thought of that, good idea," Lizzie replied and wrote that down in her notebook that now seemed attached to her like an extra appendage.

After they cleaned up the dishes, they took Lucky and Ella for a walk down to Alhambra Hall. It was now used for parties and receptions and was very popular as it looked out over the water into Charleston Harbor. The sea breeze had indeed made the air more bearable and the sun was finally slipping away.

Aunt Dorothy sighed, "I miss taking walks after dinner with your Uncle George."

"I can't imagine the depth of your loss. I was looking at the calendar and I realized in September it would have been your fifty-sixth anniversary," Lizzie responded.

"Yes, we had been together really fifty-nine years. My parents made us wait a while to get married. They wanted to be sure that I finished college. We met at the end of my freshman year and his junior year. Uncle George was two years ahead of me and after he graduated he also did a tour of duty in Vietnam, and once that was completed and he was released, we set the date," Aunt Dorothy explained.

"How did you know he was the one?" Lizzie asked. "That's easy; he made me laugh, he was honest and I could look in his eyes and see love looking right back at me," Aunt Dorothy answered.

"I think the mistake I made with Mark was that I didn't really think on that level. I mean ... he met the criteria I had set. The expression that comes to mind is ... and he looked good on paper," Lizzie admitted.

"Well child, I think you have learned a valuable lesson. I don't think you will make that mistake again. Love does not meet a set of criteria, it doesn't follow a rational path, and it just is, when it's the right person. You will know it when you find it. You won't need to change who you are fundamentally. Although for marriage you will have to compromise, it is no longer you but us," Aunt Dorothy elaborated.

"That is another thing that was wrong with my marriage to Mark. There was no us, just a him," Lizzie said. "I'm sorry, we started out talking about you and Uncle George and I turned it back to me and my problems," she added.

"No need to apologize, child. I am glad you are feeling more comfortable talking about what is going on with you. Your Uncle George would be some pleased that you have taken steps to turn your life around and he would be tickled pink about The Biscuit Box. I would not be surprised if he is the guardian angel making things happen for you," said Aunt Dorothy.

"I have no doubt about that!" Lizzie exclaimed. Both women were comforted at the thought as they turned around to stroll back to the house.

~

The next couple of days were a whirlwind as Lizzie tried to knock things off her to do list before the summer lull around the Fourth of July kicked in. When she woke up on the morning of the Fourth and took stock of where she stood, she was pleased to see her plan to open by late August was still realistic.

Lizzie came down stairs in white shorts and a red tank top already in the holiday spirit. The Fourth of July was one of her favorite holidays. She loved the food, especially the hot dogs. She loved the music, parades, the beach and the boats but most of all she loved the fireworks. This year she was looking forward to an afternoon on the water with a picnic dinner and anchoring near Morris Island to take in the magnificent fireworks display that was launched each year from a barge near the Yorktown at Patriot's Point.

She and Aunt Dorothy worked together to make a butter bean salad, a shrimp salad and mini-corn muffins. Lizzie also created individual red white and blue trifles in clear plastic cups with white cake, strawberries, blueberries and a luscious white chocolate cream. While they worked they tuned into their favorite musical "1776". They grilled hot dogs for lunch and spent the early afternoon talking about Aunt Dorothy's upcoming trip. Around three they packed up the coolers and the boat bags with their creations, drinks, and towels, and perhaps way more things than they actually needed and waited for Mr. Lee to collect them. It seemed strange Uncle George was not with them and they both missed him acutely.

Mr. Lee drove them to the marina where his boat "Lady Justice" was waiting and ready. Mr. Lee was fortunate enough to belong to a Marina where a staff got your boat ready when you wanted to take it out and cleaned it up for you when you came back to the dock.

"The captain grants all permission to come aboard," Mr. Lee said helping Aunt Dorothy on to the deck.

Lizzie turned to see Mrs. McGantry coming down the gangplank with a wide brimmed hat and a blue sundress covered in white stars. "I see I'm just in time," she said as Mr. Lee offered her his hand. "Tommy, I am so pleased you asked me to join you. The fireworks are my favorite part of this holiday. I can't wait to see them from the water!" she said.

Lizzie had never seen Mrs. McGantry quite so girl-like. She was friendly, and seemed flirtatious with Mr. Lee. Interesting. "Dorothy I brought the book I was telling you about. You may want to read it on the plane."

"Why thank you, Marie, that was very kind of you," Aunt Dorothy replied.

Mr. Lee took the boat out into the Cooper River and headed out towards Morris Island. The waterways were quite congested but everyone was in good spirits and it did not take long for them to find a spot to set anchor and await the show.

They dined on the feast Aunt Dorothy and Lizzie had prepared and chatted about everything and anything as they waited for the summer sun to sink down in the west so the fireworks could begin. As the darkness began to envelope the crowd, Mr. Lee tuned into a local radio station that was playing uninterrupted patriotic music to coincide with the fireworks. Collective oohs and aahs traveled on the breeze as their eyes gazed heavenward and the sky lit up with the magic that stirred the souls of almost every American from the smallest child to the senior citizen.

Later that night as Lizzie climbed into bed she reflected on how the holiday was almost perfect. Almost since Uncle George was missing and since she had spent it without a significant other. Next year she vowed, one of those things could be rectified. It was time to move on from Mark, *but how?* She would need to put herself back out there. Just the thought made her stomach do flip flops and her palms began to sweat.

M.A. might have some ideas. *How can I even consider adding romance to the mix?* She did not trust herself to recognize the good guys from the not so good guys. Maybe she should concentrate on one big change at a time. The Biscuit Box was enough for now. As she drifted off to sleep, images of food, Bennett, and strange men paraded through her mind in a discombobulated and surreal tableau. Thankfully, she would not remember it in the morning.

Chapter Nine

It was already mid-July and The Biscuit box was beginning to take shape. Shelving for products and refrigerated cases had been installed and Lizzie had painted black chalkboard squares on several of the walls. She planned to use them to post specials. She had drafted some menus and order forms. She marveled at how much she had accomplished in such a short time and also at how enjoyable it was to work, when that work fed your soul. She was currently awaiting the sales rep for a coffee and tea supplier and was working through painting tables for the porch and some for inside.

Tom Lester walked in just as she was washing up her brushes. "Perfect timing," Lizzie said, as she dried her hands off and turned to meet her coffee and tea salesperson. She felt herself blush as she took in his blonde surfer hair and large, liquid-brown eyes that brought to mind melting chocolate. It had been so long since a man had stirred butterflies in Lizzie's stomach. At first she mistakenly thought she was coming down with something.

Tom was equally taken in by Lizzie's girl next door charm and her natural beauty. The spark between them was immediate and obvious to them both. The meeting took twice as long as a typical meeting with a supplier as neither one of them wanted to see it end. So after they hammered out the items and quantity his company would supply The Biscuit Box, he took a chance and asked Lizzie out for dinner and she quickly said yes. They set a date for Friday night and after he left, a bit of panic began to set in.

Lizzie quickly got out her phone and called M.A. "Help! I accepted an invitation for a date and I have no idea what I'm doing!" Lizzie exclaimed without even bothering to say hi.

"Whoa, there, a date huh and not with Bennett? I didn't see that one coming," M.A. replied. "So tell me about this fella, who is he? What does he look like? Do we know his people?" M.A. pressed and for Lizzie the panic began to reach epic proportions.

"Well, his name is Tom Lester. He has surfer dude blonde hair and luscious chocolate eyes, and he sold me a bunch of coffee and tea for The Biscuit Box. Oh, and he is the first man in I don't know how long that made me feel like I had butterflies invading my internal organs. He seemed very energetic, but other than that I know absolutely nothing about him," Lizzie told her.

"Hmmm ... perhaps you should call him and tell him you'll meet him at the restaurant. That way you will have your own car and means of escape, plus the new rules of dating also say meet someone you don't know in a public place so they won't know where you live. You know in case they're an axe murderer or something," M.A. replied.

"Good thinking," Lizzie smiled to herself as M.A.'s instincts always had her thinking of the worst scenarios.

"By the way, we put the house on the market yesterday and we already have a showing scheduled for later this afternoon. I am coming down next week to begin the house hunt. Jim and I have narrowed it down to that area north of town where Highway 41 is. That way we can be between my parents in Snee Farm and his parents out in Awendaw and both sets of grandparents can be happy," M.A. informed her.

"Great, let me cook dinner for you one night and we can hang out on the swing bed like we used to," Lizzie said. "That is a plan, now you better call me first thing Saturday with details of this date," replied M.A.

The two hung up, both feeling a warm glow in their heart as they were now fully ensconced into each other's lives. *It seems no matter what detours one takes, life has a funny way of putting you back on the path you were meant to be on all along. Or did life give us detours in order to learn lessons and fully appreciate and recognize the right path when we find it again? Either way, we end up where we belong,* Lizzie mused as she worked her way through painting numerous chairs—well, at least the first coat. She would get the second coat on tomorrow. *Sometimes,* she thought, *I over think things! I am not going to do that with Tom, or at least I'll try not to.*

Taking M.A.'s advice she found Tom's card and let him know it would be more convenient if she could meet him at the restaurant, and would he be willing to try the new wine bar and tapas place in downtown Charleston that had opened up on Upper King Street? Tom was fine with them meeting at the restaurant, but asked several times if she was sure she wanted to try the wine bar, before saying, if that's where she wanted to go it was fine with him.

∼

The rest of the week flew by with more painting, meeting more suppliers and with Mr. Smith to make sure all the required permits were in order. She tried to stay confident about the impending date with Tom and placed quite a few phone calls to M.A. seeking reassurance and advice. Lizzie fretted over everything from what to wear, to what topics of conversation to cultivate. M.A. patiently listened and gave common sense advice, like dress comfortable but pretty and stick to interests and family, but avoid politics and religion, at least until they had a few dates under their belts.

When Friday afternoon came, Lizzie went home early to spend a little time with Lucky and Ella and Aunt Dorothy of course, and then she indulged in a bubble bath and gave herself a pedicure in anticipation for her first date in almost eight years. She carefully selected a peach silk dress and paired a thin gold belt with it and again her go to braided gold sandals. She would have chosen heels but she couldn't quite remember how tall Tom was and did not want to tower over him. How crazy was it that she was going on a date with a complete stranger! Mark had been a stranger when they met at the college library, *and we all know how well that turned out*, she thought. Before Mark had been Bennett; she had known him since preschool, she couldn't even remember being nervous with him. Well, maybe the first time they kissed.

As she applied her make up her nerves ramped up and she found herself worrying about the possibility of a good-night kiss as she selected a soft and sheer pink shade of lipstick. Lizzie transferred her essentials into a small woven straw clutch and went to kiss Aunt Dorothy on the cheek.

"Don't worry child. I'll wait up for you and we can have some ice cream so you can tell me all about this young man. I have butterscotch swirl," Aunt Dorothy said as she smiled up at Lizzie.

"Well, if I'm home early it will tell you it was a first and final date, and if I am home on the later side, you will know it was promising," Lizzie laughed trying to hide her nervousness.

～

She headed out into the early evening traffic and found a parking spot in a nearby garage a few blocks from the wine bar. She had forgotten how charming downtown

Charleston can be and marveled at the changes, the growth that had transpired on King Street since she had left home. Tom was walking, or you could really call it pacing, up and down the sidewalk in front of the entrance and when Lizzie approached she could see beads of sweat clinging to his forehead just above his eyebrows. *Apparently, I am not the only one who's nervous*, Lizzie thought, and was comforted by the observation.

Tom smiled when he saw her approach and wiped his hands on his khaki's, then tentatively leaned in to give her an awkward and stiff hug hello. *Well, he dressed like a local* Lizzie thought as she made further observation, noting his button down oxford and his sunglasses dangling on his chest by the colorful Croakies so popular among the lowcountry male population, although some points off for sporting the Carolina Gamecock motif as Lizzie had been raised in a Clemson Tiger household. Not enough to declare it would not work, she would give him a chance. After all many of her friends were in successful mixed marriages, which is what people called the unions between Carolina and Clemson households.

The hostess seated them at a table by the window and explained how the tapas menu worked and asked for their drink orders.

"I'd like a glass of Malbec, Argentinean if you have it," Lizzie replied.

"I'll take coffee," Tom said.

As the waitress turned away to fetch the drink order and give them time to look over the menu, Lizzie teased Tom by saying, "Coffee, really I would have thought you were the type who could leave your work at the office."

Tom looked very uncomfortable and gave a weak laugh, "Well you know workaholic and all."

The waitress returned with the coffee and the Malbec and took their food orders. They picked an assortment of small plates to share. Lizzie was looking forward to the pear slices with manchengo cheese and honey the most. She told Tom how jealous she was that her Aunt Dorothy was going to get to taste food all over the globe. He shared how he had traveled extensively in South America for surfing and had learned to eat a lot of new things on his adventures. Lizzie noted Tom's hand was shaking as he tried to raise his cup to his lips and he had to use his other hand to steady himself. He stared at Lizzie's wine over the rim of his cup like a red tailed hawk getting ready to swoop in on his prey.

"Are you alright?" Lizzie asked as she began to bring the wineglass to her lips.

Tom sat down his cup on the saucer with such a clatter it drew the attention of the couple at the next table. "I wasn't going to tell you this so soon but I'm actually a recovering alcoholic," Tom admitted reluctantly.

Lizzie took a moment to weigh her response carefully; her choice of words would make or break this date. She pulled her wine glass a little closer to her and looked him in the eye and said with a nervous laugh, "Well, I guess my suggestion for a wine bar was not the way to go."

Tom seemed to visibly relax that she took it so easily and maybe in hindsight relaxed a little too much as he began to tell her the tale of how he became an alcoholic and how he struggled with his demons on a daily basis. Lizzie grew more and more uncomfortable as she tried to nonchalantly sip on her wine. She tried to imagine being able to enjoy a drink in his company and knew this was going to be a big problem.

They made an awkward attempt at conversation. Lizzie asked about his people, but apparently he came from a family with alcohol and substance abuse issues, so that just added to the awkwardness.

Lizzie told him a little about her soon to be ex-husband, but that was just a downer on the evening. Finally they stumbled on the fact that they both enjoyed watching and reading mysteries. They both had enjoyed the PBS series *Sherlock*, which set the world renowned detective in modern times. When they had exhausted that topic they lapsed into an uncomfortable silence.

The wine bar began filling up with more patrons and the alcohol was flowing all around them. Before Lizzie could protest, the waitress brought a fresh glass of wine and then whisked off to another table. *Where is the food?* Lizzie wondered as they continued to sit in awkward silence. Lizzie got the feeling ice cream with Aunt Dorothy was going to be quite early.

While Lizzie contemplated how to graciously extract herself from this disastrous date, *note to self: always have an escape plan*, she glanced over at Tom and got the sense he would end it, before she could come up with a plan. She did not have to wait long for it to play out.

Tom nervously glanced around the room registering all the drinks in his sight like the pictures that line up in the slot machine windows in Vegas. He nervously tapped the table with his fingers and his leg was jiggling up and down. The sweat now cascaded down his face, dripping from his nose. His hands were trembling and Lizzie thought at any minute he was going to crawl out of his skin or go into cardiac arrest. That would be something, a date ending with an exit provided by EMS.

Then suddenly he swooped his hand across the table and grabbed up the new glass of wine and before Lizzie could even say stop, he had guzzled it down, the wine seeping out and down his chin and on to the front of his shirt. He looked across the table at her, his eyes wild and crazed as if they were not really seeing her. This time he attracted the attention of most of the tables around him as he let out a primal scream and leapt out and ran out the door heading for the bar across the street.

Lizzie, with as much dignity as she could muster, as the whole place was now staring at her, weakly said, "Check please." It was all she could do to hold her head up high and walk back to her car as if nothing had happened. She considered going after him to see if she could help, but realized she would probably make things worse.

Once she was back in her vehicle she called M.A. "You are not going to believe what happened," she started. By the time she had told the whole story to M.A., M.A. had laughed so hard she had to put down the phone several times before she could regain her composure.

Thirty minutes later when she arrived home Aunt Dorothy said, "Guess this one is not a keeper. I'll get the ice cream."

Aunt Dorothy could not keep a straight face as Lizzie spilled the details. "Oh, I do hope he is alright ... It's a shame to be so young and already have such a cross to bear," she said when Lizzie had finished.

"I'm beginning to think I just attract the wrong kind of man," Lizzie confessed.

"No, child, I don't think that's it. I think you expect the better of people and sometimes don't see beyond the surface, but in this situation I think you met a nice young man who was trying to turn his life around, but unfortunately wasn't there yet," Aunt Dorothy reassured her.

Lizzie sighed and rested her forehead on the table. "I think this calls for a second bowl," Lizzie mumbled.

Aunt Dorothy patted her head and said, "I'll get the carton."

Chapter Ten

"Well, I must say, Lizzie, this place is looking impressive," declared M.A. as she took in the almost finished space of The Biscuit Box.

"Thanks!" said Lizzie "I have been working day and night and we are only ten days away from the grand opening. Here, look over the menu. It will change seasonally and I will have a weekly special also."

M.A. looked over the menu and her stomach began growling. "I guess that means you like it," laughed Lizzie.

"Yes, I want one of everything! I don't know if I can wait ten days!" M.A. replied.

"You will only need to wait eight days, as you are on the friends and family trial run lunch service. I hope you can be back here from Virginia then," Lizzie answered.

"I should be able to. Jim is already here living with his parents as his new job has started. I did my final shift at the hospital last week and to keep the house ready for showings the girls are here too, bouncing back and forth between the grandparents. So I don't intend to go back to Richmond until the house sells and I need to get it all packed up. Before we head out for dinner tell me more of the setup here," M.A. requested as she looked over the shelves of local products and cookbooks.

"Well, besides serving brunch and lunch at the tables, there is a menu to order take home and bake casseroles, tomato pies etc. and of course pick up to go biscuit boxes with flavored butters and jams. There is the shopping section you're looking at featuring all kinds of regional products, grits, Carolina rice, tea, pickles, etc. Some of the products won't be here until the end of the week. I can put together gift baskets with the products and my food made right here in the kitchen. Also, I have a menu of classes for kids and adults that will be on Saturdays through the fall," Lizzie explained.

"How are you going to manage all this? Are you going to work twenty-four-seven?" asked M.A.

"Well, initially I will have to work a lot, but I have hired two trained cooks from the community college's culinary arts program and I have some part-time servers/ shopkeepers. One of them is Laura Collins, who I baby sat back in the day," Lizzie answered.

"Wow, Laura is old enough to have a job? I guess that makes sense since we are old enough to be parents and employers," M.A. commented. "Let's head out and get dinner, I can't get my tummy to stop rumbling," she added.

"Okay, let me lock up and we need to run by the house real quick to take the dogs out and change. I'm a little grungy," Lizzie replied. While Lizzie changed, M.A. took the dogs out back with Aunt Dorothy.

"No conspiring against me!" Lizzie hollered as she headed up the stairs."

"Conspiring? Who us? We promise to only trade notes on your progress," M.A, hollered after her.

Thirty minutes later the two friends sat sharing a platter of boiled shrimp and knocking back some beers. "Thanks for agreeing to eat out, rather than our original plan for me to cook back at the house. My work hours are a little out of hand right now," Lizzie said.

"No worries, you know I always like hanging out at Reds on Shem Creek," answered M.A. The two sat out next to the dock in view of the shrimp boats that lined the creek. Lizzie had just arranged for one of the local shrimpers to be her supplier. The sky was painted with swirls of red, orange and pink as the day slipped into evening and all around a mix of locals and tourists enjoyed the break in the heat as the sea breeze stirred up.

"So, how is the house hunting going?" Lizzie asked. "Well, we saw a charmer in Darrell Creek. It had nice wide porches like Aunt Dorothy's house, and inside it had the more modern open plan. I really wanted to put in an offer, but Jim is nervous about the risk of having two mortgages. He thinks we need to wait until the Richmond house sells, but I'm worried we will lose out," M.A. explained.

"I still can't believe Mount Pleasant now reaches that far up Highway 17 or that the new high school up that way is so huge!" Lizzie commented.

"It is a little surreal, but I love the idea of the girls attending our high school, even if it is a different building," said M.A. "Now, I know your first attempt to get back into romance was a little rocky," M.A. began.

"A little rocky! Let's call it a complete failure such as it was. I was humiliated sitting in that bar and I was horrified for Tom. I felt like I literally pushed him off the wagon! Did I tell you a replacement rep showed up at The Biscuit Box and informed me Tom had gone away on an 'extended vacation,' code for off to rehab I am sure." Lizzie raised both of her hands, palms upward.

"Well, I don't know if you can call it a complete failure. After all you took a chance, you went through the motions, and I think it is time to try again. You know, before you let your experience get the better of you." M.A. pulled off a shrimp's shell like a pro.

"And where am I going to meet anyone if I am up to my eyeballs in opening this business?" Lizzie dipped a shrimp into cocktail sauce.

"I have a plan for that, and I won't take no for an answer. Jim has a college buddy, a guy named Coleman Reed who went to the Citadel with him. They were not best buds or anything, but Jim ran into him when he was switching our car registrations back to SC and he thought he would be a good match for you," M.A. explained.

"Why, pray tell, would Jim think this guy is a good match for me?" Lizzie pushed the platter, now piled high with shells over to where the waitress could easily retrieve it.

"Well, for starters he is down to earth, not stuffy, he was very active back in the day, running, tennis and I believe he has two golden retrievers just like you. To make it a little less stressful, we thought we could double, just some friends meeting for drinks. What do you say?" M.A. looked hopeful and Lizzie found that as usual it was too hard to say no to M.A.

"What do I have to lose?" Lizzie answered. *At least she didn't try to push me at Bennett again.*

"Great, Jim will set it up and we can go from there." M.A. drained her beer and smiled.

The two friends sat, staring out at the creek. They ordered more shrimp and beer and sat for another hour as the sun slowly slid down and the summer night air blanketed them. As they sat, they talked about the kids, M.A.'s possible new house, Aunt Dorothy's impending trip and Lizzie's impatience with the divorce process. She did enjoy telling M.A. that Mr. Lee had sent a formal letter to Mark about the issue with the mail, and since then, an envelope full of mail had been sent to her.

"So what did you and Aunt Dorothy discuss in the yard?" Lizzie's curiosity finally getting the best of her. "Well ... she is tickled pink about The Biscuit Box. She wishes you would come to your senses about Bennett and she worries about you being alone while she is off gallivanting around the world," M.A. told her.

"And what did you add to that?" Lizzie asked.

"I said, ditto, ditto, ditto and then I promised to look after you," M.A, laughed.

"Well, at least you want good and not evil for me. I think you two are a force to be reckoned with," Lizzie said, taking it all in stride.

~

After the friends parted ways, M.A. went home to get Jim moving on the date with Coleman and Lizzie, feeling restless, headed back over to The Biscuit Box to do a little bit more work, calling Aunt Dorothy of course so she would not worry.

Lizzie unlocked the back door and turned on the kitchen lights. She decided she would make up a batch of benne wafers to drop by Mr. Smith's office since he had pushed through the last of the permits and she wanted to thank him. She grabbed an apron from the hooks along the wall by her office and tied it on. She went to the fridge and pulled out the long log of dough that had been chilling. She set the oven to preheat and began to slice coin sized wafers and placed them on a Silpat lined baking sheet. She would need to take some home to Aunt Dorothy as well; she adored having benne wafers and tea in the afternoon. She was working along rhythmically when the hair on her neck stood up and she felt her heart beat fast as she heard the sound of the front door of the store open.

It was dark in the front of the store. She had come in through the back. Yes, she heard steps that seemed to move cautiously on the floor coming towards the kitchen. Lizzie looked around in panic and grabbed the cast iron pan sitting on the counter. She crept towards the door taking care to angle herself behind it, her back to a storage shelving unit. Suddenly the door swung open and Lizzie simultaneously lifted the pan overhead, underestimating its weight and instead of swinging it towards the intruder, the pan pulled her back, knocking into the shelving unit behind her. A plastic bin pitched off the shelf and showered Lizzie head to toe in fluffy white flour.

Stunned, both she and the intruder stared at each other and then the intruder burst out laughing, "Lizzie, what the hell ..."

"Don't you what the hell me! Bennett what are you doing here? You about gave me a heart attack!"

"I was down the street when the security company alerted me the silent alarm had been triggered, so I used my key and came into check the system. That's when I saw a light under the kitchen door. Did you forget to enter the code?" Bennett asked.

"Um. Yeah, I came in through the back. I completely forgot I had set the alarm when I left before." Lizzie looked at Bennett sheepishly. It galled her to no end that once again he was catching her in a less than stellar moment. With all the dignity she could muster she stood up and got the broom and dustpan.

Bennett promptly grabbed them from her, "I'll sweep, you go get yourself cleaned off," he said.

Without a word Lizzie stepped out the back door and shook off all that she could. Why did it seem that every time she had an encounter with Bennett, losing her dignity was par for the encounter? She returned to see Bennett had even gotten out the vacuum to finish the job.

"Thanks, Bennett, I promise to be a more responsible tenant and be more careful with the alarm," Lizzie said as she kept her eyes on the counter, again afraid to look him in the eye.

"No worries, it looks great around here. I can't believe how much you have accomplished in such a short time. I will definitely be at the friends and family trial run next week. Thanks for including me."

Lizzie looked up at him briefly and saw he was smiling at her and she relaxed a little. "Since you're here, do you want some iced tea, while I finish baking this tray of benne wafers?" Lizzie offered.

"Thanks, but I was on my way to meet someone. I'll take a rain check though," he said.

Lizzie followed Bennett to the front door to lock it behind him, promising him that she would set the alarm before she left. She watched from the dark storefront as he pulled away. *I wonder who the someone is he's off to meet?* Immediately, Lizzie chided herself for caring. *After all, I've already declared that my relationship with Bennett is not to be resurrected beyond friendship. Then again, why did I make that declaration?*

She felt her cheeks burn as she remembered the night they had broken up a decade ago. She had informed him that now that she was off to college and he was staying home to go to college here, they needed to end things. She was off to find a man with a plan, who had some ambition. She felt guilty as she recalled how judgmental she had been of Bennett and now look, he was a successful business man and she had little to show for investing in a "man with a plan."

Lizzie sighed and went back in the kitchen and finished baking her benne wafers. Her mind wandered back to Bennett and curiosity or ... was it jealousy that he had gone to meet "someone," a girlfriend perhaps?

When she got home and took the dogs out she checked her phone and found two text messages. One from M.A., they were set for Tuesday night to double date and the other message was from Bennett. It said, "Lizzie you are one of the most responsible people I know. The Biscuit Box will be an instant success."

Lizzie smiled and texted back a simple, "Thanks."

~

The preparation days were a blur of vendors, printers, and planning for the friends and family trial run on Wednesday and the grand opening on Friday. So, pleased that all was finally in place, Tuesday late afternoon she locked up and set the alarm and headed home to get ready for the promised double date, grateful for the distraction and the knowledge she would have friends along.

She chose a pair of white capri jeans and a royal blue cotton tunic trimmed in green piping and she went with a silver sand dollar necklace and silver drop earrings. Once again, she slipped the emerald cocktail ring over her wedding ring indentation, which seemed to be getting less pronounced, or was that wishful thinking she mused as she slipped on her sandals and went down to chat with Aunt Dorothy.

The two enjoyed a few moments while waiting on M.A. and Jim to pick her up. Aunt Dorothy was making a list of what she still needed to get for her trip and kept Lizzie entertained with details of the itinerary she had just gotten from the travel agent. Lizzie made her promise to leave a copy for her, to which Aunt Dorothy assured her she would. Their conversation turned to Lizzie's second foray into the dating game.

"Have fun, and remember to look at his eyes; that will tell you what you need to know," Aunt Dorothy called after her as Lizzie dashed out to Jim's car.

"The eyes, got it," she hollered back, although she didn't quite buy into Aunt Dorothy's long standing belief that a person's eyes could reveal the contents of their character.

As the four settled into their table and gave the waitress their drink orders, she was relieved when Coleman ordered an adult beverage without batting an eye or breaking out into a sweat and as they all looked over the menus she took a moment to study him. He had dark hair that was thinning a bit at the top and he had long eyelashes. He was tanned and fit.

He glanced up at her over his menu and as she briefly looked in his eyes, she was startled by what she saw, or correction what she did not see. His eyes seemed veiled, lacking any emotion.

Okay, this train of thought is ridiculous. I'm inferring way too much and probably unfairly due to Aunt Dorothy's parting words. She smiled at him and he smiled back revealing perfectly even, (braces in the past), and extremely white, (must use bleach) teeth. She turned her attention back to the menu and told herself she would give Coleman a fair chance.

As the evening progressed they discussed their work, the changes to the area since Coleman and Jim had graduated from the Citadel and even ventured into politics. He was looking more and more promising and Lizzie relaxed even more.

"So Lizzie, Jim tells me you are getting divorced ... " Coleman was saying as they were left alone at the table; Jim and M.A. had not so discreetly excused themselves one to the restroom and one to call the babysitter to check in on the girls.

"Divorced! I'll tell you who is filing for divorce, me," shrieked a woman with a baby strapped to her back and a toddler clutching her hand, looking like both were ready to cry.

"Lucille!" Coleman began to try and calm the woman, but she continued her tirade and the surrounding tables had gone pin drop quiet.

"A business dinner, I don't think so. I read your email about your double date. This is the last straw Coleman. I forgave the fling with the babysitter, I took you back after you hooked up with that bimbo on our beach trip, but no more ... "

Lizzie sat shell shocked, and Jim and M.A. who had returned to the table as they heard the commotion, stared open-mouthed at Coleman and the woman who was apparently his wife and the mother of his children. Coleman stood and mumbled an apology and corralled Lucille and, by this time, his crying children out of the restaurant.

M.A. said, "Jim, how could you not know he was married?"

Jim began sputtering, "I took him at his word."

Lizzie looked from one to the other and slowly put her head down on the table, getting some of the sauce from her plate in her hair.

M.A. patted her on the back. "Sit up, Lizzie, people will stop staring if we just act natural," M.A. coaxed.

Lizzie quietly sat up and said, "Get me a bourbon and ginger and we are definitely getting dessert."

"Ah, Lizzie, tonight is on me and I guess I am paying for Coleman too," Jim added.

"Let's not mention that name again sweetie," M.A. shot Jim a look that told him he was going to hear way more about this when they got home. The three ate dessert, paid the bill and Jim and M.A. took her home.

Aunt Dorothy looked at her as she walked in the door and said, "I guess he was another dud."

"You could say that," Lizzie replied, "You were right about one thing, his eyes were a good clue."

Chapter Eleven

Aunt Dorothy sat back in her chair, setting the stack of response cards she had been reviewing on the table next to her. "Well, child the feedback is overwhelmingly positive but that is no surprise to me considering the passion you have poured into The Biscuit Box," she said as she smiled at Lizzie.

Lizzie was stretched out on the sofa responding to the emails and texts she had gotten from many of the guests at her friends and family trial run. "Yes, things went really well today and several people ordered take-away casseroles for pick up on opening day. I just hope I get customers off the street on Friday," Lizzie yawned.

"I reckon you best get to bed early tonight. You will have a lot to do tomorrow to get ready for Friday," Aunt Dorothy commented.

"I don't think I could sleep a wink. I am still buzzing from today. I think I'll take the dogs for a walk down to the old bridge and back."

"Alright child, I will most likely turn in while you're gone. I want to start that book Marie McGantry gave me on the Fourth of July."

Lizzie leaned down and gave Aunt Dorothy a kiss on the top of her head as she headed to the kitchen to grab the leashes.

"Take your phone with you," Aunt Dorothy called after her.

"I will," Lizzie hollered back and she looped back into the den with the dogs in tow and scooped the phone up off the sofa. With the dogs eagerly pulling her out the front door as she headed down the street.

The dusky light of early evening cast long shadows through the majestic oaks that dominated the yards, the storybook moss gently dancing in the breeze. The streets were lined with charming cottages and stately homes, graced with inviting porches.

At one time Mount Pleasant had been a small village to the neighboring city of Charleston and even into the early 1990's it had retained its small town charm. Although the town had exploded in population and sprawl north along highway 17, the Old Village retained the charm one expected from a small southern hamlet. The scenery had not really changed since Lizzie's childhood, with the exception of the refurbishing of the homes, most owners respecting the history and architecture of their properties.

The heat of the day had given way to the warm eighties' and the breeze made the humidity bearable, all in all a pleasant night for early August. Lizzie contemplated the progress she had made since returning home. Her divorce was still pending, but she realized she had not really thought about Mark in any significant way in weeks and if she was really honest with herself she was not even heartbroken about his exit from her life. She had to admit she was angrier and more hurt by her inability to see him for who he really was and she was slowly forgiving herself for that. Uncle George was a hole in her heart that was slowly healing. She missed him terribly. She would have liked him to have been one of the friends and family at the trial run today, but in a way, she felt he had been. She had thought about him and felt him warm her heart.

She had been touched by the sweet story Bennett's niece had shared with her about Uncle George teaching her Sunday school class how to mend a shrimping net, it was tied into a lesson on how the disciples had been fisherman. The class had then taken a Sunday afternoon outing down to the old bridge to cast their nets and Uncle George had taught the kids how to shrimp and crab.

Bennett ... how sweet that he had brought his niece to the trial run as his lunch date. He really was good with kids. Despite her misgivings about him being her landlord, he had been very supportive and had given her a little more latitude with the property than what an average landlord would have, or at least that is what she suspected, not having vast, no correction, any experience leasing commercial property.

That thought led her mind to The Biscuit Box just as she reached the railing of the bridge. It technically was not a bridge, it used to cross over from the edge of the Old Village to Sullivan's Island. It actually supported a trolley service, but had been dismantled in the 1930's. Eventually the town had created a little recreation area that allowed for fishing, crabbing and shrimping into Cove Inlet and had a view across to Sullivan's. Lizzie had spent hours here with Uncle George as a child and was entertained by the tales her grandmother had told of riding the trolley for beach outings as a child.

She took in the view which was quickly fading as the night sky took over, but she could make out a pair of porpoises swimming up toward the Inter-Coastal Waterway. Her dream of her own business was becoming a reality. It was still a risk, she would need more than friends and family for customers, but the write-up the Moultrie News had published this week had been a great opportunity for free advertising and she had gotten a call from the principal of the elementary school in the village wanting to place a large order of biscuit boxes to have at the faculty's back to school meeting for teachers. *I should print some coupons to send with the order.*

Lizzie took a deep breath and attempted to put work thoughts on the back burner. The moon had begun to rise and it was almost full. The moonlight shimmered on the water, casting a spell. Lizzie stood mesmerized by its beauty until the dogs, who were growing impatient, began to tug on their leashes. Lizzie began the walk back, the dogs now on an even pace as their excitement about the walk had settled.

So taking stock, the only part of her life she was unhappy with was her love life. What love life? It was pretty much non-existent and her two dating experiences made her hesitant to hold out much hope that a Prince Charming was going to drop from the sky and sweep her off her feet.

Poor Tom, he had issues but the one thing she gained from the experience was that she had broken her inertia by going on a date. You can't swim if you don't get wet, isn't that what Uncle George used to tell her when she was afraid to try something? And Jim meant well, he took an old college buddy on his word, it wasn't his fault Coleman had been a lying, unfaithful bastard.

So I guess I will have to be open to try again, Lizzie thought, *but not until I get this business rolling.* She took the dogs in, hung up their leashes and filled the water bowl. Then she went back to read the response cards once more. She lingered over the card Bennett had filled out ... *The best shrimp salad I have ever had! That's saying something, as you have tasted the one my meemaw makes. Can't wait to be a regular! Do you think you could make those pecan tassies you used to make?*

Lizzie took it out of the stack and headed upstairs to get ready for bed. She rummaged in her desk drawer and found some transparent tape. She affixed Bennett's card to her mirror, just like she used to do with ticket stubs and pictures when they were still a couple. She crawled in to bed making a mental note to add pecan tassies to her baking agenda.

~

Friday seemed to arrive in a blink of an eye and Lizzie arrived to unlock and bake up fresh biscuits at seven o'clock. At nine o'clock she had a steady stream of customers that did not let up until ten-thirty. She barely had time to work with her new cook Zoe, to make up some tomato pies and shrimp salad before a lunch crowd began and when the next lull occurred around one-thirty she had accumulated a stack of take away orders for the next week along with some gift baskets.

She was glad she had hired a few helpers, but if this pace kept up she would need to hire at least two more. She was also glad she had opened on a Friday, which gave her Saturday to be open, but closed on Sunday so she could regroup for the six day week to come.

Mr. Lee had brought a client for lunch and Mr. Smith had gotten biscuit boxes to take to the office in the morning. Bennett and his sister had come in and had brunch and M.A. had brought the girls in for the pimento cheese plate and to order a casserole for tomorrow. Even Mrs. McGantry had come with some of the ladies from the altar guild. Plus quite a few people had read about the opening in the paper and come to check it out.

When the day was done, Lizzie realized she had been on her feet for over twelve hours. It would not always be like this, but she wanted to be there for her seven to six business hours at the beginning, coming in before and staying after until she was confident in her staff and how things were running.

She had locked up after she had posted the cooking tasks for the morning and she took a list home of supplies she needed to order, thank goodness she could do so on-line and also that her receipts were electronically filed. Lizzie sank down into the recliner and sighed in relief as she elevated her feet.

"Here child, I made you a fried egg sandwich," Aunt Dorothy said as she placed a small plate in Lizzie's lap and gently pushed Lizzie's hair away from her eyes.

"Thank you, how did you know I hadn't eaten?" Lizzie asked.

"I know you child, you were too caught up." Aunt Dorothy smiled and then with a look of concern in her eyes added, "I hope you don't intend to keep this pace and these hours, you need to have some balance in your life too."

"I know Aunt Dorothy, I definitely will need to hire a few more workers. I think I need to find an accountant to help me keep track of the books also. I don't want to do paperwork, electronic or otherwise every night," Lizzie answered.

"Why don't you talk to Amy? I think she was an accountant before she had her third child. She might know someone," offered Aunt Dorothy.

"I'll do that," Lizzie yawned. "She did tell me she did books for some businesses and I know she does Bennett's." Lizzie yawned some more. "I better take the dogs for a walk before I fall asleep." Lizzie and the dogs went for a short walk around the block, then realizing she was too tired to tackle the computer work, she quickly crawled into bed.

~

The first few weeks kept a similar routine but as Lizzie was able to hire a few more part-time workers and got the rhythm of the rushes and lulls of the customers she began to feel comfortable coming in at seven o'clock and leaving between three and four. The dining spaces were only open nine to one with the other hours for pick-ups and sale of products only. She had decided to put off the cooking classes, realizing she had enough on her plate for now. As August rolled into September, she had cultivated a core group of regulars and had new customers discovering her place every week.

It was also time for Aunt Dorothy and Maggie to go off on their around the world adventures. Lizzie perched on the end of Aunt Dorothy's bed and watched her finish her packing on the eve of her departure. "I know you will have a great time, but I am sure going to miss you," Lizzie handed Aunt Dorothy a stack of blouses.

"I am so very excited," Aunt Dorothy replied. "But with the Skype you set me up with on that tablet you insisted I take with me, we can see each other now and then and I promise to email at least every other day."

"I am reassured by that, I have been spoiled though with you having dinner for me every night since I opened the business," Lizzie said.

"Well you need to promise me you won't just work and hang out here, all work and no play will make Lizzie a dull girl. You need to spend time with your friends and maybe find someone special," Aunt Dorothy lectured.

"You sound like M.A. Both her and Amy have been on me to get back out there," Lizzie shared.

"How is Amy working out with the books?" asked Aunt Dorothy.

"She is so efficient, and she has had some good suggestions on how to better negotiate with my suppliers. She has a good head for business. It must run in the family," Lizzie answered and found herself thinking of Bennett.

"Hmm ... any more thought to Bennett? You could consider trying to rekindle things with him. That would make your Uncle George very happy," probed Aunt Dorothy as if she had read Lizzie's mind.

"Guilt will not make me go down that road. Besides, I think he might be involved with someone, and I don't think he wants to be more than friends. He hasn't made a move to ask me out since I've been back," Lizzie answered.

"Could that be because you have held him at arm's length with your attitude towards him? Honestly, I never understood why the two of you split. If you really look at him ... I mean look deep into his eyes, I think you would see there is something still there, if you aren't too afraid," Aunt Dorothy boldly stated.

"I ... I ... well I'm not afraid, I just don't want to move backwards," Lizzie sputtered.

"Child, just because Mark was a mistake, that doesn't mean everyone in your past is one too. Alright I can see this conversation has gotten your knickers in a twist, so I will table it for now, but when we are communicating back and forth from across the globe I want to hear that you are being social and getting out there," Aunt Dorothy chided.

"Yes ma'am, I will do my best. Now let's go down and cook your last home-cooked meal together. I picked up some shrimp on the way home," Lizzie said. The two women enjoyed a final quiet evening together cooking and soaking up each other's company.

~

The next day Lizzie saw Aunt Dorothy off to the airport. She would meet up with Maggie in Atlanta. For the first time in weeks, Lizzie felt an uneasy loneliness settle over her. Driving back to the shop, their conversation from the night before paraded through her brain, and like a slap across the face, she realized, *I would want to try again with Bennett. I'm not afraid, I'm ashamed that I ended things the way I did. Besides he doesn't want me, so that ship has sailed. I need to resolve to move on.*

As she pulled into her parking spot and headed into the kitchen, she pushed all thoughts of Bennett out of her head, or at least that is what she told herself. Bennett was making that fairly difficult as he had settled into the habit of stopping in daily, for coffee and biscuits or sometimes for lunch. She found herself watching and waiting for his appearances and looking forward to the light-hearted exchanges between them. Their friendship was slowly re-kindling and Lizzie suspected that Bennett was as pleased about it as she was. Still, she could not bring herself to tell him how badly she felt about how she had treated him all those years ago and it hung there between them an obstacle neither one of them could figure out how to overcome.

Chapter Twelve

The humid days of September whirled by and reluctantly relinquished their grip on the Lowcountry. It was finally October, football season was in full swing. It would be at least a month before any leaves turned colors in the early morning there was a hint of crispness to the air as Lizzie rode her bike down to The Biscuit Box. Soon it would be too dark to ride her bike, but this morning she was enjoying the carefree feeling pedaling to work.

Amy was coming by to update the books after she got her kids off to school and before she had to run and pick up the two youngest—Charlie and Faith, from the pre-school. Lizzie had adjusted her menu to reflect some of the seasonal changes and was looking forward to seeing how her regular customers would respond. She had replaced several salads with a crabmeat casserole with toast points, a gumbo, and butternut squash bisque. She had switched out the fruit butters that accompanied her biscuits for a pumpkin butter, a sweet potato butter, and a cranberry butter and she had also added a warm apple cider to the drink choices. She had barely been in business for two months and if the projections for the next few weeks were accurate, she would turn a modest profit by the time the calendar rolled into November.

Amy arrived at nine o'clock and got right to work in the small office off the kitchen. When Lizzie could step away from the front she brought Amy a mug of her favorite chai tea and a warm scone.

"Yum, thanks," Amy said. "I looked over the menu changes. I definitely need to bring mom by. She is wild about butternut squash," Amy continued.

"I remember her being a fan of most soups too," Lizzie replied.

"You know she is pleased as punch about you being back here. I think she is hoping you and Bennett will find your way back to each other." Amy looked at Lizzie trying to gauge her reaction.

Lizzie sighed. "I don't think your brother has any interest. Besides who can blame him? I was so judgmental and snobby to him when we broke up."

"I don't think he sees it that way, but then again he keeps his matters of the heart to himself. I just want the both of you to be happy," Amy responded.

"I appreciate that. I've not exactly been batting a thousand in the romance department," Lizzie said.

"I heard. M.A. felt so bad about what happened, but she and I do agree we need to help get you back out there. So if my brother is off the table, I have a guy I would like you to meet. His name is John Ayers and he has his own computer repair business. I've done the books for him for the last two years," Amy said.

"What makes you think we would be a match?" Lizzie asked.

"I don't know that you are, just that he is a nice guy. I do need to tell you he had an ATV accident about five years ago and has a prosthetic leg as a result. He was a little sensitive about it when I first met him, but now he seems much more comfortable. You would not necessarily notice if you weren't looking for it," Amy explained.

"Well, what have I got to lose? I did promise Aunt Dorothy I would keep getting on with life while she was gone. It would be nice to have something to tell her in one of our email exchanges," Lizzie smiled.

"Great! We are planning to get a group together to meet at Red's to watch the Clemson-Georgia game on Saturday. That would be a low pressure way for the two of you to meet," Amy said.

"Okay, I will mark it on my calendar," Lizzie answered, and allowed herself to feel a glimmer of hope.

~

Later that week, Mrs. McGantry came in for lunch. "Lizzie, dear this crab casserole is divine!" she exclaimed.

"Glad you like it, Mrs. McGantry," Lizzie answered. "I had a wonderful email from your Aunt Dorothy. What a hoot! The train worker strike in Spain had them taking a bus into France in the wee hours of the morning," Mrs. McGantry continued. "I wanted to ask you a small favor my dear. I have plans to go with a friend up north to see the fall leaves and my Sweet Pea, that's my cat, will need someone to check in every few days to put fresh food and water out, give her a few pats. Can I count on you?" She asked using the same tone and expression that got everyone to participate in the annual church bake sale, even folks who didn't know a scone from a turnover.

Lizzie knew she could earn major points with Mrs. McGantry if she said yes, but was also worried she would somehow not care for Sweet Pea to the caliber Mrs. McGantry would expect. As she hesitated, she heard Uncle George's voice in her head saying to her, "Kindness costs nothing to give, but is worth more than all the riches on the earth."

"Of course, I would be glad to look in on Sweet Pea," Lizzie answered.

"Thank you so much dear. On Saturday I'll bring you a key and a list of instructions," Mrs. McGantry said as Lizzie headed back to the kitchen to check on the casseroles she had going in the oven.

On Saturday, Lizzie opened the shop and Mr. Lee came in for coffee and biscuits. "Do you want your usual chicken and rice casserole on Wednesday?" Lizzie asked as she rang up his purchases.

"Not this week, Lizzie. I'm headed out of town. Be back next weekend though. See you then."

Lizzie watched as he headed out the door. Was there a little pep in his step? Shortly after, Mrs. McGantry arrived with a four-page, typed list of instructions and the key to her house. "I know you will just love my precious Sweet Pea. She has quite a few years on her, but she is my heart. I can't imagine not having her around," Mrs. McGantry gushed.

"I will do my absolute best and follow your instructions to the letter," Lizzie answered.

"I knew I could count on you dear. I am leaving tomorrow afternoon and will be back on Thursday night. Got to run! Have so many more things to do before I jet off." And with a wave of her hand, Mrs. McGantry sailed out the door with an energy Lizzie had never witnessed from her before.

"Well, who would have believed that?" Laura said as she wiped down the counter next to Lizzie. "I didn't think that woman had a cheerful bone in her body."

"One thing I've learned lately, is you never know how a person can be or how they can change," Lizzie replied, smiling. *If Mrs. McGantry can go from stuffy to cheerful, then I can go from shallow to looking beneath the surface.*

As the brunch crowd faded away, Lizzie went over some afternoon pickups with Laura, and then headed home to take the dogs out and make a quick change. It was almost time to head over to Red's on Shem Creek before the big game, and meet this nice guy, John Ayers. It was still quite warm, so she wore sandals with her blue jeans and put on a Clemson shirt so there would be no mistaking for whom she was rooting.

~

The sky was a deep autumn blue and small wisps of white clouds drifted above, not shielding anyone from the intense afternoon sun. Amy and their crowd were gathered near the bar on the dockside deck in sight of several televisions broadcasting the pre-game hoopla. Pitchers of beer had been ordered and an assortment of appetizers was being debated when she walked up.

"Hey, glad you could make it," Amy said.

M.A. came up on her other side and leaned in for a hug. "Good news, the house in Richmond is under contract for twenty-thousand over the asking price, so Jim and I put in an offer on the Darrell Creek house," she said.

"That is great news! I'll keep my fingers crossed that you will get it," Lizzie responded.

Jim, Scott and Bennett were debating the merits of the starting line-up and the performance of the teams so far this season, boldly making predictions of what all the stats meant for the outcome of this game. Bennett turned and gave her a wave. She waved back and whispered to Amy, "A little awkward meeting someone new with Bennett here."

"Well maybe it will get my little brother to realize the great opportunity he is missing," Amy whispered back. Before Lizzie could respond, Amy was calling out, "We're over here, John."

Lizzie turned to see an auburn haired, broad shouldered man walking towards them. She felt herself blush. She could not see his eyes because he had on aviator sunglasses, but she imagined they would be green. Amy took care to introduce John to the guys first and then on to the girls, saving Lizzie for last. They found themselves smiling at each other and chatted about the game and the weather and lots of typical social conversation. John quickly drained his beer and grabbed another out of the bucket he had ordered when Lizzie excused herself to the restroom.

M.A. followed her. "So what do you think?" she asked.

"I think he is a nice guy. Don't know that I can say any more than that," Lizzie answered.

"I guess that's fair. I hope third time is the charm," M.A. replied.

When they rejoined the group, John had drifted over to the guys and was intently watching as the second quarter came to an end. He was deeply engaged in conversation with Bennett and Scott about sports. I guess he's not interested, Lizzie thought. She was sitting at one of the tables the group had commandeered on the deck when John came over and joined her.

"So, Bennett tells me you are new to the small business world," he said.

"He is correct about that," Lizzie said, and felt herself flushing at the idea Bennett had discussed her with him. Wanting to steer the conversation away from anything he may have discussed with Bennett, she began to extol the virtues of the Clemson quarterback, who was leading the team with two touchdowns over Georgia.

"Yeah, he can do all that, and I bet most men here could do some of the same, but none of them can do this," John interjected. Without any warning, he reached up the leg of his shorts, removed his prosthetic, grabbed the pitcher of beer from the table, emptied it into his leg and proceeded to guzzle down the beer.

The talking around them ground to a halt. Although a roar had erupted on the other side of the deck as Clemson scored another touchdown, their crowd did not even notice. All eyes were on John and Lizzie.

"Um, was it something I said?" Lizzie whispered.

John pushed his sunglasses up onto his head. His eyes looked angry and were not the green she had imagined, but a brown that was not chocolate but more like deep mud.

In a sarcastic voice, John mimicked her, "Was it something I said.' Look lady, there is more to a man than how he can run and perform on a football field."

"B ... but I was just talking football. I wasn't judging you!" Lizzie sputtered, her cheeks burning. M.A. swooped in to move her away. Bennett moved towards John, laying a hand on his shoulder.

Lizzie heard him say, "Hey buddy, I think you have had enough. Let me drive you home." Then she could not hear anymore as Scott and Jim had circled around blocking her view and her earshot. A short time later, with his leg restored, John was helped out to Bennett's truck and taken home. Jim followed in John's car.

"Well strike three and I'm out," she said to M.A. and Amy.

"No, you can't give up that easy," M.A. said.

Amy concurred and added, "Just you wait. A great love is still around the corner for you, you'll see."

Lizzie gave them a weak smile. "Somehow I doubt that, but I am so glad I have friends who can continue to cheer me on despite my disastrous track record." As Clemson ran down the clock for another win, Lizzie headed home and drowned her sorrows in a large bowl of caramel ice cream.

~

After work on Wednesday, she swung by Mrs. McGantry's for the last time. She would be home tomorrow and so far taking care of Sweet Pea had been a breeze. Her only concern was the cat, who had not touched her food. Maybe she was just missing her human. After all, Lucky and Ella had been known to do the same on the rare occasions she had been away from them.

When she opened the door and Sweet Pea went streaking by her and sought cover under the holly bush in the side yard, Lizzie was taken by surprise. Sweet Pea was an indoor cat and until now had shown no interest in what was going on outside her door. Lizzie left the door open and went to check the food and water. Again, nothing appeared to be touched. She went back to the door and tried to coax Sweet Pea back inside—first calling her, then trying to entice her with treats.

After an hour, Lizzie was losing patience. Sweet Pea was more obstinate than ever, settling deeper under the prickly leaves. Lizzie sighed, and spoke to the cat. "Okay have it your way. I will put your food and water bowls here by the door and come back in a couple of hours to get you in for the night." Seeming to understand, the cat let out a pitiful meow.

Lizzie rode her bike home and after supper and walking the dogs she jumped in her car and headed back under a starlit sky. The air was definitely on the chilly side and she pulled a sweatshirt over her head. It would definitely help protect her from the holly leaves if she had to get in the bush to get Sweet Pea back inside. The food was still untouched by the door and she could see Sweet Pea sleeping under the bush. She called to her, but heard no response. She moved in closer, shaking the branches gently—still no response. Lizzie felt a pit of dread develop in her gut. She reached in and touched Sweet Pea. No response. Sweet Pea seemed oddly stiff. Lizzie leaned down and shone a flashlight onto the cat's face. The edge of Sweet Pea's tongue was protruding out of her mouth.

Lizzie jumped back. Oh my God! I've killed Mrs. McGantry's cat! I will never be in her good graces again. I will have to close the store and move to Siberia to escape her wrath. She paced in and out of the house, unsure of what to do next. Then, without really thinking about it, she found herself calling Bennett.

"Bennett, help. Oh my God. I have done something horrible. You've got to come and help!"

"Slow down, Lizzie, where are you?"

"I'm at Mrs. McGantry's."

"On my way," he said and the line disconnected. Ten minutes later, he found her pacing on the sidewalk in front of the house. "What happened?" he asked, seeing the distress on her face.

"I ... I killed Sweet Pea! Now I will have to move to Siberia! I don't want to move! I don't want to close the store! I'm going to have to break my lease ..."

"Back up, who is Sweet Pea?" Bennett asked.

"Mrs. McGantry's cat. I was cat-sitting while she went on a trip. I knew I should have said no, but Uncle George ... oh, never mind. What should I do? She will hunt me down and kill me!"

Bennett started to laugh. He tried to control it, but soon was doubled over and hooting as if she had just delivered some amazing stand-up routine.

"Stop it Bennett! This is not funny!" Lizzie yelled at him.

Bennett managed to get himself back in control. "Lizzie, I thought you had done something more serious, like killed Mrs. McGantry—you know, finally losing your cool with her condescending ways ... although lately she has been awfully friendly. Anyway, I thought her cat died years ago. She got that cat way back when we were in grade school! It must have been ancient."

"I can't believe you think I could commit murder! I don't care if Sweet Pea was around for the Civil War. Mrs. McGantry will never forgive me."

Lizzie's distress was so palpable that Bennett pulled her to him and hugged her, kissing the top of her head. "I don't think it will be as dramatic as all that. I think I have one thing we can do that will help."

He released her and made a call to one of their old high school classmates, who was now a vet in his father's practice.

After a short conversation, Bennett got a towel from his truck and carefully wrapped Sweet Pea in it. He placed the cat in the bed of his truck.

"Michael will examine Sweet Pea and determine the cause of death. He can store the body until we find out if Mrs. McGantry wants Sweet Pea buried or cremated. Come on, Lizzie, lock up and I will follow you back to the house. We can go see Michael together. Tomorrow, I will wait here with you to meet Mrs. McGantry when she gets home."

"Why are you so good to me?" Lizzie mumbled half to herself.

"Has it ever occurred to you I might still care about you?" Bennett blurted. Then he backtracked. "Your Uncle George would expect no less from me. Come on, let's go.

We shouldn't keep Michael waiting. He's coming into the clinic just for us."

Lizzie sighed, locked the door and drove back to park her car before getting into Bennett's truck. It was going to be a long night.

Chapter Thirteen

Lizzie and Bennett sat in silence on the steps in front of Mrs. McGantry's door. Both looked at each other in surprise as Mr. Lee's car pulled up with Mrs. McGantry in the passenger seat. Mr. Lee and Mrs. McGantry exchanged a hand caught in the cookie jar kind of look as Mrs. McGantry said, "I wasn't expecting a welcoming party ... um ... Mr. Lee and I met up at the baggage claim and he graciously offered me a ride home."

"I am not sure how to tell you this," Lizzie began. Before she could continue, Bennett jumped in.

Taking Mrs. McGantry's hands in his own, he gently led her into the house and sat her down in a chair. Still holding on to her hands he knelt down to be at eye level with her. "I regret we have to tell you, Sweet Pea has gone to heaven. Dr. Brown, Jr. examined her and told us it was her time. There was nothing Lizzie could have done to prevent her passing. Her record showed she was twenty-two years old," he gently explained to her.

McGantry's eyes misted over. "My poor Sweet Pea! Dr. Brown, Sr. did tell me she had outlived her life span and it was common for cats to go away or wait for me to go away to pass on," she said.

She is taking this better than I thought she would. Thank goodness Bennett is here to handle this.

Mr. Lee sat beside Mrs. McGantry and placed his hand on her back. "I'm sorry, Marie. I know how much you loved that cat," he said.

Mrs. McGantry smiled at him, "I really did, but everything has its season." She glanced back and forth from Lizzie to Bennett. "Nice to see you two as a team," she added.

Lizzie blushed and Bennett suddenly developed an interest in studying the pattern on the living room rug.

Mr. Lee said, "I'll stay with Marie. You kids run on."

Out on the sidewalk, Lizzie turned to Bennett. "Thanks Bennett. You really had a gentle touch with her. I know that made all the difference."

"You're welcome. You know Lizzie, no matter what, I'll always have your back. All you have to do is call." "Good to know," she replied. "That goes both ways, you know."

"Good night Lizzie. See you around." Lizzie watched as Bennett got in his truck and drove away before she headed home. If she could only be brave enough to tell Bennett she wanted much more than back up.

She could not wait to email Aunt Dorothy and tell her all about the cat calamity.

～

The next few weeks were fairly routine with the exception of her twenty-ninth birthday and a surprise delivery from France from Aunt Dorothy.

"I can't believe she sent me authentic French baking molds!" she exclaimed to M.A., who had arrived at The Biscuit Box with a cupcake, complete with a lit candle to make a wish. Lizzie closed her eyes, thought of Bennett, wished with all her might and blew.

"So ... what did you wish for? That was a pretty intense expression you had on your face," M.A. observed. "You know better than to ask. If I tell you, my wish won't come true," Lizzie sassed.

The door jangled. Lizzie looked toward it ready to greet her customer, but was surprised to find herself face-to-face with Bennett. "Hey, Bennett." She tried to keep her voice casual while her heart pounded up into her ears. *Had M.A. rigged that cupcake with a magic candle?*

"Hey Lizzie ... M.A. I need a coffee and a half dozen of your pecan tassies to go please," he said, reaching for his wallet.

"Coming right up," Lizzie answered reaching for a bag for the tassies.

"Oh, and Amy asked me to invite you for Thanksgiving. She said she won't take no for an answer. She has collected Mr. Lee and Mrs. McGantry too. You won't be the only holiday orphan at the table. Oh, and happy birthday," he added.

"Okay, I guess I'm coming for Thanksgiving. Tell Amy I will call to see what I can bring." She handed Bennett his change, tassies and coffee.

M.A. had stood there observing the exchange and when Bennett had departed, she turned to Lizzie and said, "I don't have to ask what you wished for. I think it just came true!" She gave Lizzie a quick kiss on the cheek and waltzed out before Lizzie could protest.

～

The two weeks that led up to Thanksgiving were slammed with extra orders for biscuit boxes, side dishes and casseroles with the majority of the pickups being the afternoon before Thanksgiving and Lizzie found herself back to twelve hour days. She had found time to touch base with Amy and get her assignment for the Thanksgiving feast, an oyster dressing for the dinner and spiced pecans for the cocktail hour. She had also told Lizzie to bring Lucky and Ella, as all family should be together on the holiday. So Lizzie had stayed up late Thanksgiving eve to make the pecans and prep for the dressing so she could lounge in her pajamas and take in the Macy's Parade.

She was over the moon when the phone rang and Aunt Dorothy was on the other end. "I can't believe you are calling all the way from Greece!" she exclaimed.

"Child, Thanksgiving is a day for family and I am missing you so much! But I will tell you we are continuing to have a grand time, Maggie even tried the grappa. I am so glad you will be with Bennett today," Aunt Dorothy said.

"Well, it's not with Bennett. He will be there, but it's at Amy's house." Lizzie tried to sound nonchalant.

"It sounds like you're splitting hairs, child. Be thankful for this opportunity to rebuild the bridge between you. And I don't want to hear you're not interested, or he isn't. I think I know the two of you better than that. Listen, got to run. We are catching a boat to see some of the islands. Love you to the moon and back," Aunt Dorothy declared.

"Love you too! Send more pictures," Lizzie replied, and hung up the phone feeling so thankful to have the best aunt in the world.

Lizzie finished preparing the oyster dressing and donned a gray tropic weight wool pencil skirt and an emerald green silk blouse. She put on what was becoming her signature emerald jewelry and took extra care with her makeup and hair. Then stowing the dressing in a cooler to keep curious canine noses out of it, loaded the food and the dogs in the car and headed for Amy's house.

The afternoon was pleasantly passed with appetizers, cocktails and preparations for the main meal. Lizzie helped in the kitchen as naturally as if she were a member of the family. It was so nice to spend some time with Bennett's mom and Memaw.

"I hear you make a shrimp salad to rival mine," Memaw said.

"Yes, ma'am ... I mean no ma'am, not unless you believe your grandson is a qualified food critic," Lizzie stammered, not wanting to presume her cooking could truly be superior to that of a woman who had been cooking longer than Lizzie had been on this earth.

Memaw reached over and patted Lizzie's hand. "I take no offense. My family has been bringing me samples of your delectable creations for months now and I whole-heartedly agree with my grandson's assessment. You, Lizzie Long, are a gifted cook."

Lizzie flushed with pleasure. "Thank you ma'am. That means more to me than you could possibly know," Lizzie answered. Memaw was renowned for her culinary skills much like Aunt Dorothy.

"Well, we know you can out cook me," chimed in Mrs. Wilson. They all laughed. It was no secret the cooking gene had skipped a generation with Bennett's mom. She was known for burnt offerings that frequently set off the smoke detector.

"That's okay Mama. No one can smock as adorable a dress as you," Amy reassured her mother.

"Thank you darlin'. At least I mastered some of the domestic arts," Mrs. Wilson replied. The four women put the finishing touches on the feast and called the men folk and the children to eat.

Amy had a dining room table that accommodated most of her guests but she also had a second table set up in the formal living room. She had place cards at each place and had conspired to place Bennett and Lizzie at the secondary table along with the kids. After they had gathered around the main table to hold hands and say the blessing, Bennett and Lizzie helped the children get situated with their plates.

At first Lizzie felt a little self-conscious, but soon Bennett had her in stitches as he told tall tales and made puppets out of the napkins to entertain his nephews and niece.

Jeremy, Bennett's mini-me nephew, got particularly wound up and in an impulsive moment. He flicked a spoon of mashed potatoes at his big brother Charlie, who promptly responded with a spoon of his own, Charlie's aim was poor and he hit Bennett instead, who gleefully joined in flinging potatoes across the table hitting Jeremy square in the nose. They were all laughing now and Jeremy reached his hand into the bowl of potatoes on the table, scooping a fist full just as Bennett stood up to move around the table and gain some control over the situation before Amy could blow her cool.

She was already hollering from the dining room, "What's going on?" As Bennett moved behind Lizzie's chair, Jeremy launched his potato volley and it landed on Lizzie's forehead and slid down her face and onto her blouse just as Amy and Scott stuck their heads in the door to see what all the noise was about.

Lizzie turned multiple shades of red and began to shake, Bennett looked at her, waiting for the explosion of anger, but instead she swiped her face with her finger and licked it, declaring, "Tasty!" Then she burst out laughing. The rest of the table began to giggle uncontrollably and Amy and Scott joined in, unable to keep stern faces. Although they did decide to make Jeremy apologize to Lizzie and removed the tempting bowl back to the sideboard.

Lizzie took a quick shower and borrowed some clothes from Amy. This seemed to be the norm for a visit to the Hutchins' house. She rejoined the group in time to gather in the den to eat dessert and enjoy some coffee. It was wonderful to feel part of the family. It felt great to not be worried about her image, as she had been on all the Thanksgivings she had spent with Mark, not with family but as guests at the homes of potential political backers.

She sat back and watched as Bennett alternately rubbed Lucky and Ella's belly, as Scott and Amy were affectionately interacting with their kids and Mrs. McGantry was laughing at some story Mr. Lee was regaling her with. This is what a holiday should be. It wasn't Norman Rockwell; it was better. It was genuine and she wished with all her heart the Thanksgivings in her future would be no less than today.

~

The day after Thanksgiving launched a holiday season like no other Lizzie had experienced. She was swamped with orders and had to hire a few seasonal workers to get through the crunch. On a Tuesday in the middle of the holiday whirl, she had just finished a marathon session of gift basket assembly in the afternoon lull and looked up when she heard the customer door jingle and found herself looking directly at Mark.

Immediately she felt her shoulders tense and her temple begin to throb. Mark did not speak at first but with an assessor's eye took in the shop and then a long appraising look at Lizzie herself. "What brings you to town?" Lizzie heard herself saying, marveling at the control she heard in her voice.

"Darlin, I thought I ought to check in and see how you're doing," Mark replied. Lizzie found it hard to resist the urge to gag.

He was laying it on thick. He must want something, *Red Alert, Red Alert* flashed across her brain. "As you can see, I am just fine. Did you want to make a purchase or are you just browsing?" She struggled to keep the sarcasm out of her voice.

"Lizzie ... I think I was a little hasty to not give our marriage a fighting chance. You see, you really are the girl for me. Besides, now that you have access to some funds, we can go all the way to the governor's mansion ... what do you say baby, you can't possibly want to waste your time in this little shop for the rest of your life?" Mark said, ignoring her question.

"I can't even believe you have the gall to say that to me, let alone show your face here! Are you really that arrogant, Mark? Did you really think now that I have some money—which by the way is all mine since we are legally separated—that you could get your grubby paws on it? Why would I choose to come back to you?" Lizzie ranted incredulously.

"Darlin', you can't do any better than me. Without me you will amount to nothing. I see you still have not mastered the art of self-control ..."

Mark suddenly went quiet. Lizzie felt a strong hand wrap around and rest on her shoulder. She looked up to see Bennett quietly staring Mark down. He did not speak to Mark, but asked Lizzie, "Everything alright here? I wouldn't want to upset our little bun in the oven."

Lizzie's eyes grew wide. She looked from Bennett to Mark. Mark sneered and said, "Not surprised you would get yourself knocked up. I can see I am wasting my time here. I knew you weren't first lady material, but I'll admit your inheritance was motivation to try and make a go of it." Mark sneered as his fake charm faded, revealing the cold and calculating man he truly was.

"I can see a quick divorce is the only option we have left." And with not so much as a "have a great life" or a "sorry for messing up your life," Mark turned on his heel and strode out of The Biscuit Box. Lizzie blinked back tears, not for losing Mark, but for the years he had stolen from her.

Bennett gently kissed her on the top of the head, "Told you, I will always have your back."

"A bun in the oven ... That's how you have my back? Though the look on Mark's face was priceless. How did he know about my inheritance?" Lizzie said.

"I'm sure it came out in prep for the divorce, and when he realized the only way he could get his hands on it was if you reconciled, he felt compelled to give it a go."

"Well I can't wait until the ink is dried on those divorce papers and I can officially be Lizzie Long again."

"You will always be Lizzie Long to me," Bennett murmured, and slipped back through the kitchen door.

Lizzie stood still for a moment grateful the shop was empty. She turned to go after Bennett. Entering the kitchen, she called, "Wait ... why are you here?"

Zoe looked up from the pot she was stirring on the stove. "He just left, but he left you an official looking envelope over on the desk."

Lizzie walked over and picked up the thick legal-sized envelope and carefully opened it. Inside she found documents for a sales contract for the building The Biscuit Box was occupying. Her name was listed as the purchaser, and he was giving her the opportunity to be her own landlord.

Lizzie held the papers close to her heart. It was over-whelming to know he believed in her with no strings ... or was he cutting the strings of their landlord-tenant relationship with her because he didn't want to have any obligations to her? *I sure wish Aunt Dorothy was here*, she thought. *Am I over thinking this?* Before she could contemplate any further the shop door jangled and she plastered on a smile and stepped out to greet her customer.

Chapter Fourteen

The weeks between Thanksgiving and Christmas had been a whirlwind, Lizzie had even hired three seasonal helpers just to keep up with the gift basket orders and two more to help between the kitchen and the storefront. So when Christmas Eve arrived and she closed the shop two hours early, she indulged in an afternoon nap. Lizzie was careful to set the alarm. She was afraid that once her head hit the pillow she would not wake up until Christmas was over.

When the alarm went off she groaned, regretting for a moment that she had promised M.A. she would spend the night over at her house. It took a great deal of effort to haul herself to an upright state. She took a quick shower and dressed for the midnight service they would attend at church. Then she packed up some festive pajamas, along with a set of clothes for the next day. Once she had gathered her toiletries, she packed up bowls and food for Lucky and Ella and loaded them and all the stuff in the car.

She was grateful that M.A. had not asked her to cook or bake anything, but she knew she would help out in the kitchen once she was there. She was excited that she would be present to watch the kids open their gifts. She especially wanted to see the reaction of her godchild, Elizabeth, to the children's cookbook and adorable apron set she had found.

Now that M.A. and Jim had moved into their new house, they announced they would host the holidays and if the grandparents wanted to see the grandchildren they would come there. The days of running between and eating two dinners for every holiday were over. M.A. and Jim had laid the law down and were amazed at how easily the two sets of grandparents had agreed. At least it would work until their respective siblings got married and had children. Lizzie arrived to find the house in the throes of cookie baking for Santa.

"I'm so glad you are here!" exclaimed M.A. as Lizzie got the dogs set up with their bowls.

"It'll be fun. I can't wait to watch the kids tomorrow," Lizzie replied.

"Now at least for tonight I want you to relax and no working in the kitchen. I am sure you are exhausted. I have supper for tonight well in hand. Hopefully it will meet your culinary standards, and I even have a breakfast casserole in the fridge ready to bake for breakfast," M.A. informed Lizzie.

Lizzie gave her a grateful look. "I am exhausted. I never really knew how hard it is to work in retail during the holidays."

Once M.A. got the cookie decorating cleaned up and the girls off to play, she finished up her prep for their supper. The two friends relaxed with some hot tea.

Jim came in, giving both women a kiss on the cheek. "Mission accomplished."

"What's he talking about?" asked Lizzie.

"Oh, you will see tomorrow morning. We have a big surprise for the girls," M.A. explained.

After supper the five of them went over to the church for the midnight service. The air was crisp and the girls enjoyed huffing their breath to make mini clouds in front of them. The walkway up to the church was lined with luminaries and the arched doorway was surrounded by evergreens and twinkle lights. Inside, the church was dramatically decorated, draped in garland and wreaths of evergreen and magnolia leaves. Candles burned in the windows and some small fir trees with simple white lights flanked either side of the aisle. Lizzie was enthralled with the beauty, but taken more by the looks of wonder on the faces of the girls, and all the folks young and old around her.

She saw the Hutchins and Wilsons and waved. Jeremy ran over and gave her a quick hug before joining his siblings in their pew. After the service, they all met outside, Scott carrying little Faith and Jim carrying Rebecca, as both toddlers had fallen asleep during the service. Greetings and hugs were exchanged and Lizzie found herself lingering in a bear hug from Bennett.

"Merry Christmas, Lizzie," he said, and gently kissed her on the cheek.

"Merry Christmas, Bennett," she replied, touching his cheek with her hand.

"Hurry up, we've got to get home and hang our stockings," declared Ben, the oldest of Amy and Scott's children. All the other kids, at least those who were still awake, chorused, "It's stocking time! Santa Claus is coming to town!" On that note, the families said goodbye and headed home.

Once the stockings were hung, Lizzie climbed into the grand rice bed M.A. had in her guest room, visions of children and Bennett dancing in her head.

The next morning was a hurricane of wrapping paper and shrieks of delight. Lizzie was pleased that Elizabeth was enthusiastic about her cookbook.

"Miss Lizzie, you can teach me how!" she had squealed.

Lizzie was surprised that there were several gifts for her from Aunt Dorothy. "You are not the only one Aunt Dorothy has emailed from across the world," M.A. explained, as she noted the look of surprise registering on Lizzie's face when she handed her the first package.

Aunt Dorothy had wrapped gifts from different countries and shipped them to M.A.'s house. Lizzie received a wool plaid scarf from Scotland, a box of chocolates from Belgium and a delightful wood carved angel from Germany. She had also sent Elizabeth and Rachel each their own magnificent wooden marionette puppet also handcrafted in Germany. To M.A. and Jim she sent a stunning nativity set from Spain.

After it seemed all had been opened and appreciated. Jim said, "Now there is one more surprise. I will need to go next door to get it, so hang tight." While he went to fetch the mysterious gift, Lizzie, M.A. and the girls cleaned up the wrapping paper and neatly stacked each person's gifts into discernible piles.

Jim came in with a large basket that had a blanket covering the top. Lucky and Ella perked up, sniffing the air and their tails began to wag furiously. Jim carefully sat the basket down and pulled back the blanket. He reached in and lifted out a small bundle of wriggly fur.

"A puppy!" the girls squealed.

"Not just any puppy," Jim explained. "This is a Boykin Spaniel, the South Carolina state dog. She is ours; we just need to figure out her name."

The rest of the morning was spent watching the antics of the puppy as she interacted with the girls and Lucky and Ella. By the time Lizzie and her four-legged children returned home, she found she was rejuvenated. She was ready to tackle the remaining work to get the holiday season to New Year's Eve.

~

Lizzie looked into the camera and smiled, "You look fantastic, Aunt Dorothy," she exclaimed as a bright-eyed Aunt Dorothy looked back at her via the computer screen.

"Child, I feel fantastic, but pardon me for saying so, you look exhausted," Aunt Dorothy replied.

"I am. I closed the shop at twelve today. The holiday season has been non-stop. Thank goodness we made it to New Year's Eve. It's only two, in the afternoon, and I have already changed into my pajamas," said Lizzie.

"We are getting ready to head out to supper. They eat late here in Italy and tonight there should be festivities and fireworks to boot. We are gussied up and plan to be out past midnight, I'm surprised you aren't going out with friends tonight. New year, new start Lizzie," said Aunt Dorothy.

"I am just too tired. Believe me both Amy and M.A. have been on my case about staying in tonight, but I want to end this year on my own. There will be time to start anew tomorrow, I'm going to Mrs. McGantry's for Hoppin John and collard greens," answered Lizzie.

"Oh, I'm glad of that. I have had some entertaining emails from Marie recently. Well I need to say, arrivederci and Buon Anno, that's Happy New Year in Italian! I'll post new pictures tomorrow and remember Tuesday we take off for a four day jaunt in Egypt," Aunt Dorothy said.

"Be careful! Keep emailing, our next scheduled Skype is two days after you arrive in Australia. I love you and give my best to Maggie," Lizzie declared.

"Will do child, will do," and blowing a kiss Aunt Dorothy signed off. Lizzie shuffled back to the couch to find a good movie to get lost in.

She started a fire in the fireplace and the dogs were soon sacked out in front of it. She pulled up the soft chenille throw, not because she was cold, she just wanted the comfort factor of snuggling underneath it. She had stocked the coffee table with some cheese wafers, salted almonds and bottled water. Lizzie clutched a steaming mug of hot cocoa and had indulged herself with some whipped cream to top it off. With the remote in hand she settled in for the afternoon.

She found one of her favorites, a black and white classic called *Arsenic and Old Lace*, a delightful Cary Grant film. She woke up with drool escaping the corner of her mouth, the credits rolling and the phone ringing.

"Hello?" she said groggily.

"Well, hell. Did I wake up the biscuit queen from her afternoon nap?" laughed M.A. on the other end of the line.

"I just dozed off during a movie. What's up?" Lizzie rubbing the drool off her chin.

"Just wanted to check and see if you changed your mind about joining us tonight," asked M.A.

"No, I really want to stay in and say goodbye to this year my way," Lizzie answered. Feeling the need to explain she continued, "I have been through a lot this year—Uncle George, the end of my marriage, a total upheaval of my life. Not to say the last year has been all bad. After all, I finally am following my dream. I have reconnected with my best friends and I am back home. I just want the year to end on a quiet note. Besides, I think I would need toothpicks to hold up my eyelids if I even attempted to socialize tonight."

"Okay, just thought I would try ... see you next year!" M.A. said as she acquiesced to Lizzie's wishes.

After hanging up, Lizzie went in the kitchen and made scrambled eggs and toast for dinner. She carefully rebuilt the fire in the fireplace. Once the fire was steady, she fetched her wedding album and took out the pictures one by one. She watched them burn, the edges curling at first, then the whole picture disintegrating into ash. She kept two photos, one of Aunt Dorothy and Uncle George as parents of the bride and one of her and Uncle George cheek-to-cheek on the dance floor. It was a close up so you couldn't even tell she was wearing a wedding dress.

Then Lizzie found every photo she had of Mark, which was not many as he often gave her a hard time about taking pictures unless it was a campaign worthy event, and she burned those too. By the time she was done it was nearly eight so she let the dogs out and popped popcorn, taking care to pop extra for the dogs. They were nuts for popcorn.

Once they were all settled back into the den, and she had watched some of an NCIS marathon, she looked at the list of movies in her Netflix queue and selected *The King and I*, one of her favorites. This time she managed to stay awake for the whole movie. Lizzie, caught up in the romance of it, fantasized about Bennett as the King and herself as Anna, whirling around the dance floor. As if Bennett would be caught dead in that outfit let alone channeling his inner Fred Astaire, and that thought made her smile. If she needed him to dance, she knew he would, he had finally convinced her he would always have her back. *But what about me? Does he know he can count on me? Not likely. When was the last time I did something for him?* She felt her cheeks burning as once again, she realized she was the selfish one in this relationship. She did not want to be Bennett's Mark, but how to fix it? That is one thing to put on my New Year's resolution list. I must be a better person to Bennett.

Her phone binged indicating an incoming text message. It was from Bennett. "Happy New Year," it said, and around her she heard fireworks being shot off. It was midnight. She texted back, "Happy New Year. I have your back, too." Then, afraid of what he might text back, she turned off the phone and with the dogs headed upstairs to crawl into bed.

～

"Come in! Come in!" a cheerful Mrs. McGantry greeted Lizzie at the door.

"Thank you so much for inviting me," Lizzie answered, as she handed Mrs. McGantry a jar of homemade pickles. Lizzie entered the living room and saw Mr. Lee on the sofa holding a small long haired gray kitten.

"Oh, she's adorable," Lizzie exclaimed. Mr. Lee held out the kitten to Lizzie, who promptly took her in her arms, loving the purring vibration that emanated from deep inside the ball of fluff with startling blue eyes.

"Meet Angel," Mr. Lee said, "and Happy New Year!"

"Same to you," Lizzie answered. "Seems you have been spending a lot of time with Mrs. McGantry lately, Mr. Lee," Lizzie queried.

"Very observant of you dear. Actually, Marie and I have been seeing each other lately," Mr. Lee answered.

"You have?" Lizzie exclaimed, unsure what to make of it.

"Yes we have," Mrs. McGantry said as she entered carrying a tray of iced tea, spiced nuts and cheese wafers. "You probably are unaware Lizzie, but Tommy and I were an item back in high school."

The two smiled at each other. As Mrs. McGantry sat down next to Mr. Lee, he gently took her hand in his.

"Really," Lizzie replied, "What broke you two up?" she asked.

"Well, it was silly really. Tommy was headed to The Citadel and planned to go on to law school and I was impatient to get out into the world, so we went our separate ways. I took a job as a nanny to a local family that had been called to serve in the diplomatic corps in Japan, it was a chance to go see an exotic part of the world. When I returned home, Tommy had gone off to law school at Tulane and I met my Gerald, god rest his soul, and he swept me off my feet. We got married in a whirlwind, had a few good years together and then he died in that awful plane crash. I got caught in the role of the poor sad widow and even though Tommy had returned home to open his practice, we never could reconnect," Mrs. McGantry explained.

"That is not entirely true," Mr. Lee interjected, "If you recall about twenty years ago, I tried to get you to give us another chance, but you were adamant you could not go down that road."

"Well, I felt guilty, partly because I felt I owed Gerald loyalty and partly because if I was truthful with myself I had to admit, I had always loved Tommy even when I chose to marry Gerald. He really was such a good man," Mrs. McGantry replied.

"So what changed, why now?" asked Lizzie.

"We can thank your Aunt Dorothy for that," Mr. Lee answered. "For years she had watched me pine away for Marie, not giving other ladies a fair shake."

"And she watched me sink into more misery and unhappiness over the years," interjected Marie.

"When your Uncle George died, she scolded us both, cajoling us into trying again, daring us to find a way to make each other happy and it worked," Mr. Lee explained, gazing adoringly at Mrs. McGantry.

"We were finally honest with each other, there was a reason we had connected in our youth and there was a reason we continued to care for each other all these years. I realized that Gerald would want me to be happy and most of all, I realized I could trust Tommy with my foolish heart. I hope you will be happy for us," Mrs. McGantry added.

"I'm thrilled for you both," Lizzie said with genuine affection and she felt a warmth in her heart and a hope.

"Come on Lizzie, let's get this Hoppin' John together and stir the collard greens. We need to get you some luck for the new year!" Mrs. McGantry said and she and Lizzie headed to the kitchen while Mr. Lee found a football game on the television and Angel dozed on his lap

Chapter Fifteen

Lizzie put the finishing touches on the Valentine specials flyer and then took another look at the photos Aunt Dorothy had posted from New Zealand. She and Maggie were wrapping up their tour of Down Under and heading to Hong Kong to celebrate the Chinese New Year. It was hard to believe but January was coming to a close.

How does time seem to get faster and faster? Lizzie shook her head in disbelief. The front door was jingling at a steady pace indicating the start of the lunch time rush, so Lizzie put her laptop in sleep mode and strapped on her apron. Her staff had grown so she had two workers in the kitchen and three out front the majority of business hours, freeing her to bounce back and forth between kitchen and store front as needed.

Each morning Lizzie herself would complete the majority of the orders for take-and-bake casseroles and a few extras for walk in purchases. When the kitchen crew came in they began the prep for the brunch and lunch service and an efficient routine had developed.

She stepped out of her office and made a quick survey of the kitchen. Seeing all was in hand she passed through the swinging door to the store front. It was a mild winter day so the tables on the porch were two-thirds full and all but one table was occupied inside. In addition there were several customers browsing the store and one placing a gift basket order. Excellent for a random Wednesday in winter and what really warmed her heart was recognizing many familiar faces. Repeat customers—that was a sign her business was thriving. Hers, all hers.

She had accepted Bennett's offer to sell her the property earlier than the original lease agreement had stated. She had been brave enough to ask him why he wanted to sell so soon and was relieved to find out he wanted the capital from the sale of the building so he could invest in a new boat for his charter fishing business and was not trying to sever ties with her. But still nothing had happened between them. He came in several times a week to get coffee or lunch and they made small talk.

An observer might note some effort of flirtation between them, but it never progressed past that. The longer it went on, the more Lizzie found herself hung up on Bennett. She had even lost interest in meeting anyone new, although honestly that had more to do with the three disastrous date experiences she had just endured.

M.A. and Amy had wisely backed off from trying to set her up or push her to get out there on her own.

She started towards the tables intending to check in with the customers when she heard the door jangle and turned to see who had come in. Her face lit up with a smile when she turned to see Mr. Lee and Mrs. McGantry standing just inside the door holding hands. Their faces were beaming. It was so nice to see both of them so happy. Lizzie embraced them both and led them to the free table in the dining area.

"What can I get the two of you?" she asked.

"We have several bits of business to conduct with you my dear, but first we want to indulge in some of your oyster stew before it goes out of season. I can't speak for Marie, but I want a side of your collard greens and cornbread to go with it," Mr. Lee stated, practically licking his lips in anticipation.

"I think I would like just the cornbread with my stew, so I can save some room for dessert," Mrs. McGantry chimed in.

"I will put in the order, how about drinks?" Lizzie asked.

"Sweet tea for me," Mrs. McGantry answered.

"Same for me," Mr. Lee said and with a wink added, "Although I should order unsweet to watch my girlish figure."

"Oh, Tommy," laughed Mrs. McGantry.

"Coming right up." Lizzie went to fill the drink orders herself. Mr. Lee and Mrs. McGantry lingered over their lunch and dessert not finishing until the majority of the crowd had left. They waved Lizzie over to the table and asked her to sit with them for a moment. They had something to tell, something to give and something to ask. Lizzie was intrigued and pulled up a chair.

"Well first the good news," Mr. Lee grinned and Mrs. McGantry blushed. She held up her left hand revealing a lovely antique diamond ring in a platinum setting. "We're engaged!" they said in unison and Lizzie clapped her hands together with glee.

"I am soooo happy for the two of you! When is the big day?" she asked.

"That brings us to what we want to ask. We would love to hire you to do the food for the reception; it will be a small gathering of about forty people in the church hall. We are waiting for your Aunt Dorothy's return so it will be April twenty-eighth. After all she had a hand in making this happen for us," Mrs. McGantry explained.

"How wonderful!" Lizzie exclaimed. "I would be honored and thrilled to do the food, although you do know I have never taken on a wedding or any catered event."

"We have no doubt that not only can you handle it, our guests will be so impressed, soon catering events will be another part of your business," Mr. Lee assured her.

"We will need to get our plan together. Can you stay this afternoon so we can figure it out?" Lizzie asked.

"Marie can stay, I will have to get back to the office, but before you get caught up in the merits of butter cream versus fondant, I need to present to you what we brought to give," Mr. Lee said and he pulled out an official document from his breast pocket and unfolded it. "Here is your official divorce decree. Lizzie, you are officially un-tethered and free to pursue your own love and happiness," he said.

"But, how? The year waiting period isn't done?" Lizzie sputtered in surprise.

"It seems Mark's congressional connection pulled some strings. I suspect an engagement announcement between him and a certain congressman's niece is imminent."

"Aaah ..." Lizzie sighed, "in that case, I guess I am not really surprised ... in fact I am thrilled I am finally free!" Lizzie said with glee. She felt like the weight of the world had just lifted off her shoulders. In her mind's eye, she saw Mark's condescending sneer and beady dark eyes fade out in a puff of smoke.

"Let me just say, I am also impressed you recognize the difference between butter cream and fondant, Mr. Lee," she teased. "Let me go get a notebook and some other things and we can get started on the plans for your wedding," she said as she walked back towards her office. She barely felt her feet touching the ground.

She was now officially Lizzie Long again. She was free to pursue Bennett. She never had to deal with Mark Hargrove again! Lizzie took a moment and said a silent prayer of thanks. Then she emailed Aunt Dorothy, M.A. and Amy the good news. She scooped up her big binder of recipes and a notepad and headed back out to help Mrs.

McGantry plan the menu for her reception. A reception! Lizzie felt a little nervous taking on such an important event, but she was also honored that she was trusted to do so.

Mrs. McGantry and Lizzie spent the next hour going over ideas for the menu and the cake. They settled on a shrimp and grits station, fruit and cheese display, some tea sandwiches and mini quiche as well as lemons squares, benne wafers and a red velvet cake with white chocolate cream cheese icing and they would decorate the cake with fresh flowers.

"I do think the cheese display should feature some Clemson Blue and maybe some other local cheeses as well as the classics like brie," Mrs. McGantry requested.

"Of course," Lizzie answered. Lizzie had never seen Mrs. McGantry more relaxed and friendly. She also confided in Lizzie that she had emailed Aunt Dorothy and asked her to be her one and only attendant.

"Reverend Truett will officiate the ceremony of course and I have asked Tommy's niece Eleanor to play the harp for the music, but I'm not sure who should walk me down the aisle?" Mrs. McGantry was saying as Bennett approached the two of them at the table, his eyes scanning the array of pictures of wedding cakes that were spread across the table. Lizzie had pulled up some gorgeous examples from Pinterest and had printed them up to get a feel for the style Mrs. McGantry preferred.

"Who's getting married?" he asked.

"Mrs. McGantry and Mr. Lee," answered Lizzie carefully watching his face for his reaction.

Bennett's eyes lit up with delight. "That is the best news I've heard for a while. I believe Mr. Lee has been sweet on you since Lizzie and I were kids," he exclaimed.

"Well, I guess you can say better late than never. Let that be a lesson learned," Mrs. McGantry replied, giving a meaningful glance back and forth between Bennett and Lizzie. The three paused in an awkward silence, and then

Mrs. McGantry continued, "Bennett dear would you do a crotchety old woman a favor?"

"No, but I would give a lovely mature woman such as yourself a favor," Bennett answered.

"Charming as always, Bennett," Mrs. McGantry laughed and continued, "I was wondering if you might be available April twenty-eighth to walk me down the aisle at the church."

"I would be delighted," Bennett responded taking her hand, bringing it to his lips and kissing it with a quick bow. Mrs. McGantry giggled again and rose to take her leave.

"That will be wonderful, then you can be Lizzie's escort for the occasion," she said as she quickly headed to the door and with a quick wave exited.

"I would be happy to be your escort," Bennett said, turning to look at Lizzie.

"Uh, thanks Bennett that would be great," she answered, then getting up quickly mumbled, "I've got to check on some bread I have in the oven." She quickly maneuvered herself through the swinging door then pressed her back against the kitchen wall, putting her hands up to her cheeks. They felt hot to the touch.

"You alright?" Zoe asked as she was putting away the clean pots and pans.

"Yes, Zoe I'm fine. Just catching my breath," Lizzie answered, then she headed to the office to call M.A. She would want to know this new development and Lizzie needed to hear her take on it.

"Sounds to me like Mrs. McGantry is playing match maker, and yea for her if she can accomplish what Amy and I haven't been able to," M.A. said after Lizzie had shared the events of the afternoon.

"I will say I have never seen Mrs. McGantry so happy and relaxed, or for that matter Mr. Lee as well," Lizzie said.

"That's because they are on the path they are supposed to be on with the person they are supposed to be with.

When things are aligned with the universe, it does make you happy and relaxed. Come on think about it. You might have thought you were happy with Mark in the beginning, but you were never relaxed. The only time you have been both relaxed and happy was when you were with Bennett," M.A. responded.

Lizzie stayed silent letting M.A.'s words settle and seep into her brain.

"I'm just saying," M.A. continued, "happy and relaxed are signs you are doing the right thing or choosing the right person, not that every day is a cakewalk. Did I tell you what that knucklehead love of my life did this weekend?" M.A. said.

"No, what?" Lizzie asked.

"Well trying to win the husband of the year award, he threw in a load of laundry while I had the girls out at riding lessons. He put his new red golf shirt in with light colored things. Now everything is pink, including his white dress shirts!" M.A. told the tale with her signature wit and Lizzie laughed.

When the friends hung up, she said a silent thank you to Mrs. McGantry for finagling Bennett into being her date for the wedding and also thanks to the Lord for bringing Mrs. McGantry and Mr. Lee back together again. Now she needed to email Aunt Dorothy and get her take on events and as Zoe said goodbye and left for the afternoon, Lizzie turned to computer to seek the wisdom of the person she trusted the most.

When Lizzie opened up email she found an email from Aunt Dorothy already waiting on her. She clicked and read:

My dear child,
Leaving for Hong Kong in a few hours. By now you should know that Tommy and Marie are getting married. I am so pleased for them both. If you don't know their love story, I

would press you to find out. They remind me a little bit of you and Bennett, although I hope you two don't wait until your seventies to figure it out. Maggie sends her love. I look forward to seeing your lovely face at our scheduled time once I am settled in Hong Kong. Gung Ho Fat Choy, that's Happy New Year in Chinese! I must confess that I still don't quite under-stand why they don't celebrate it on January first like we do ... hugs and kisses and pats to Lucky and Ella.
Love,
Aunt Dorothy

Aunt Dorothy had also noticed the similarities between the two couples' love stories. Lizzie could only hope she and Bennett would have a happy ending. She fired a quick email response to Aunt Dorothy, telling her how pleased she was about Mrs. McGantry and Mr. Lee, and what a great honor it was going to be to prepare the food for their reception. She told her all about the food they had selected today and how Bennett had been so gallant in agreeing to walk Mrs. McGantry down the aisle. She was careful to not respond to Aunt Dorothy's observations about the similar love stories. She was not sure she was ready to admit to Aunt Dorothy, or anyone for that matter, that she was finally willing to consider the idea of taking her relationship with Bennett beyond the tentative friendship they had established.

She powered down her laptop and stepped back out into the kitchen. "Zoe, it is such a mild afternoon. If you can hold down the fort, I think I am going to head out and take a nice long walk on the beach," Lizzie said.

"I have it all under control. You go on and I'll see you tomorrow," Zoe assured her.

Lizzie grabbed her purse and went home to change. Once again she sought the beach to help her process her thoughts and her feelings. Once again she was grateful to be home on the Carolina coast.

Chapter Sixteen

Lizzie could hardly contain her excitement; she would be collecting Aunt Dorothy at the airport this evening. She had been gone almost seven months and although they had communicated via Skype and email on a regular basis throughout her globe-trotting, Lizzie was anxious to sit across the kitchen table from Aunt Dorothy lingering over bowls of ice cream. She longed to talk with her about everything and anything. Aunt Dorothy had been back on American soil for about forty-eight hours—but had paused in Atlanta, staying at Maggie's to help ease her jet lag.

Once again Lizzie was designing a new menu for The Biscuit Box. The forsythia was blooming and the daffodils bobbed their heads indicating spring had arrived. With spring came pollen season and as the trees budded and unfurled their leaves, Lizzie reached for her seasonal medicine and kept tissues close at hand. She loved the beauty of a Lowcountry spring, but dreaded the sinus pressure and post-nasal drip it could bring if she did not stay proactive and consistent with her arsenal of relief. Even with the medicine, or maybe because of it, her brain felt fuzzy and she had a hard time concentrating on the task at hand.

The heart shaped biscuits she had offered over Valentine's had been a great success; maybe she should try bunny shaped biscuits for the Easter season? She needed to replace the heavy winter soups with some lighter ones, maybe She-crab and cream of asparagus or maybe a shrimp bisque.

She couldn't decide so she put all three on the menu. She also added a ham biscuit plate and a chutney and egg salad on croissant and took off the turkey melt with cranberry. Finally she finished up by replacing the chocolate mini cupcakes with cream puffs. The menu was complete and she emailed it to the printers. They would deliver a stack of them to her in just two days. Then she tackled the orders, only pausing to drink the herbal tea Zoe brought her along with a few cheese straws.

"Thanks, Zoe!" Lizzie hollered. The steam from the tea helped to open her sinuses and the bite from the cayenne in the cheese straws perked her up. She put in an order for some specialty chocolates to sell and put into Easter basket orders along with the never-ending supplies it took to keep The Biscuit Box running.

As she finished she yawned and stretched, ordering and paperwork were not her favorite tasks. She looked up at the clock. It was already two in the afternoon. One nice thing was that she no longer needed to draw from her personal accounts to cover expenses for the business. Over the Christmas holidays, The Biscuit Box had entered into the black and had remained steadily there ever since.

Thinking about the books of course made Lizzie think about Amy— she was so lucky to have a friend who was also a trustworthy and efficient bookkeeper.

Amy poked her head around the door to Lizzie's office space. "Here for the books," she said, "and the scoop on how you and Bennett made a date for the Mc-Gantry-Lee wedding."

"You must have been reading my mind. I was just thinking about you! I guess you have been talking with M.A.," Lizzie answered.

"Actually I heard it from Bennett. He told me he is escorting Mrs. McGantry down the aisle, but you are his date for the occasion. He asked me what I thought about that," Amy informed her.

"And what did you say?" Lizzie queried.

"I told him I thought it was the best news I had heard in a long time, plus I told him it was about time you two got on with it."

"What did Bennett say to that?" Lizzie pressed. "He rolled his eyes and told me to mind my own beeswax," Amy answered. "He also grinned and his whole face lit up at the idea of there being a two of you."

"Good to know," Lizzie responded, and felt her own face cast a glow.

"So maybe there is hope you could be my sister one day after all," Amy said as she took the seat in front of the computer Lizzie had vacated.

"One step at time, Amy, one baby step at a time," Lizzie grinned as she sauntered off to get busy in the kitchen.

She decided to leave a little early and head home to make sure all was ready for Aunt Dorothy's arrival.

Lizzie rode her bike back towards the house and found herself looking ahead ... in a few weeks it would be Easter and in a month and a half it would be time for the wedding. She had ordered the glasses and plates and such from the rental supply place, but she needed to find out if Mrs. McGantry was having the florist handle the center-pieces or did she need Lizzie to include that in her prepa-rations. When she got home, she picked up the phone and gave her a ring.

"Hi, Mrs. McGantry. How is the bride to be?" she said. "I am fabulous. I am sure you are beside yourself with

Dorothy's return. What can I do for you dear?" Mrs. Mc-Gantry answered.

"I was thinking about the tables at the reception. Do you have the florist doing centerpieces or did you need me to take care of those?" Lizzie asked.

"Neither dear. I am channeling my inner crafter. I am making the centerpieces; actually I was hoping to rope Dorothy and Pat Wilson into helping me," Mrs. Mc-Gantry replied.

"Oh, good, can I ask what the craft might be?" Lizzie inquired.

"They are glass lanterns with sand and a candle and embellished with shells and ribbon. I am going for a nautical theme, as Tommy is so fond of his boat. He is wearing white dress pants with a double breasted navy jacket and I have ordered navy with white trim table cloth toppers for all the tables," Mrs. McGantry explained.

"Sounds lovely," Lizzie replied.

"Lizzie, before we hang up, I was wondering if I could have you and Dorothy over for supper Friday night. That will give her a few days to settle in and I am sure you are tired towards the end of the week," Mrs. McGantry asked.

"Yes, I think I would be safe in accepting your invitation. I am sure Aunt Dorothy would love to see you. Would you like us to bring anything?" Lizzie asked.

"Not a thing dear. See you Friday around six o'clock. Bye, now."

"Bye," Lizzie responded and they hung up.

～

Later that night, Aunt Dorothy and Lizzie, with Lucky and Ella sleeping at their feet, sat around the kitchen table polishing off a pint of coffee ice cream and discussing anything and everything they could think of. Both of them had missed this cherished time together. Aunt Dorothy pronounced that after a day in her pajamas lounging about the house—she wanted to start putting her scrapbook together while the memories of her adventure with Maggie were fresh in her mind. She was delighted to find they had a dinner commitment at Mrs. McGantry's and she was tickled at the huge success The Biscuit Box was becoming, marveling at the article in the paper naming it along with several other businesses as the top local businesses to watch.

"I am not surprised this has been a success for you, child. After all you had your heart and soul in it."

"Thanks, Aunt Dorothy. It means the world to me to have your praise," Lizzie answered.

"Well I suppose we best get on to bed. You do have to work in the morning and I can't wait one more moment to sleep in my own bed," Aunt Dorothy rose taking her bowl and spoon toward the sink.

Lizzie got up and swooped over her, taking the bowl and spoon from her. "I'll take care of this. You go on up, and I'll be extra quiet in the morning so as not to disturb you," Lizzie said as she gave Aunt Dorothy a gentle kiss on the cheek.

"Good night, child," Aunt Dorothy said.

Lizzie rinsed out the bowls and the spoon and pulled on her sweater. She took the dogs out and walked down towards the dock. The moon and stars glistened in the clear sky. Despite the chill in the air, Lizzie felt warm to her core. Aunt Dorothy was home, her business was doing well. She even had a date with Bennett. It had taken her nine months, but she had found herself again and had a clear vision of what she wanted her future to be. Now it was up to her to make it so.

She said a silent prayer, thanking God for returning Aunt Dorothy home safely and all the blessings in her life. She also asked for intercession. She wanted wisdom and guidance to fix her relationship with Bennett. The cool air began to settle into her bones and she pulled the wrap she had around her shoulders a little tighter. She called the dogs and together they went in and locked up before following Aunt Dorothy upstairs to bed.

~

Friday night at Mrs. McGantry's, Lizzie and Aunt Dorothy got a first peek at the wedding ensemble. It was more mother of the bride in style due to the maturity of the bride, but it suited Mrs. McGantry and her nautical theme to a tee. It had a soft pleated skirt and a drop waist. The jacket had beautiful pearl buttons.

"Oh how lovely!" Aunt Dorothy exclaimed.

"Do you really think so?" Mrs. McGantry asked, clearly delighted at her reaction.

"It is absolutely perfect," Aunt Dorothy assured her. The three ladies shared a delightful supper of pan-fried flounder in a brown sauce, rice and succotash. Afterwards, they moved into the living room to have coffee and Huguenot torte.

"That was delicious. I would love to have your recipe for the Huguenot torte," Lizzie said.

"I think you already have it dear. It is in the Charleston Receipts cookbook, the one the Junior League published back in 1950," Mrs. McGantry replied.

"Yes, ma'am. I have that one and the other two they have put out. Many of my favorite recipes come from those books," Lizzie answered.

"I think I would like to be in charge of Easter dinner," Aunt Dorothy piped up. "I would like you and Tommy to come and join Lizzie and me. I promise good food and great company."

"I am sure Tommy would be delighted and I know I will enjoy the companionship with the two of you. Dorothy, did I tell you how gently and respectfully your Lizzie took care of my cat Sweet Pea in her last days?" Mrs. McGantry went on to tell her all about it and all about her new cat, Angel.

On their way home that night Aunt Dorothy said, "I truly treasured my adventures around this world, but it is good to be home ... so good to be home."

~

For Easter, Lizzie gratefully surrendered the kitchen to Aunt Dorothy who had invited Mrs. McGantry and Mr. Lee to be their guests. Lizzie served pre-dinner cocktails and cheese wafers to the happy couple as they were swinging on the porch swing. Aunt Dorothy came out between her tasks and regaled them with witty stories from her travels, having them all in stitches as she described how she used the wrong word in a Hong Kong restaurant and ended up with a fish head staring up at her from her dinner plate. After dinner, Lizzie and Mr. Lee shared the clean-up duties and left Aunt Dorothy and Mrs. McGantry pouring over the pictures Aunt Dorothy was planning to organize in her scrapbook. Occasionally they would hear peals of laughter drift into them in the kitchen.

"It is so nice to hear Dorothy laugh like that again. I was afraid after your Uncle George passed, she might not. I think Maggie had the right idea taking her off on that trip," Mr. Lee observed.

"I think so too," Lizzie answered. "It is also nice Mrs. McGantry can laugh like that too, and that is all you, Mr. Lee."

Mr. Lee smiled. "I am a lucky man, getting a second chance with my first love. I hope you, young lady, will do the same, whether it is with your first love or someone new. You deserve to have someone who brings you joy," he responded.

"I am beginning to see that," Lizzie answered as she carefully dried the silver.

"Interesting tidbit I heard at the Lawyer's Association meeting in Columbia last week. It seems Mark and his gravy train ticket tied the knot in Hilton Head last month and announced they are expecting." Mr. Lee handed Lizzie the last fork.

"Well I guess they deserve each other," Lizzie responded.

"I haven't told you the best part. The word I heard from a prominent judge in political circles, is expect the congressman uncle to be indicted on charges for accepting bribes and laundering funds through his campaign accounts. So it looks like Mark's gravy train may quickly be coming to an end and most likely with it his ability to make good on his own political aspirations." Mr. Lee began drying the silver canape tray.

Lizzie grinned and laughed a deep belly laugh and Mr. Lee joined in, flicking a dish towel at her and in a mock offended voice said, "Dear, one should not laugh at the misfortune of others." This only made the two laugh harder.

"Sounds like the two of you are having too much fun with the clean-up in there," Aunt Dorothy called from the living room.

"No more than the two of you out there," Lizzie hollered back. Then Lizzie and Mr. Lee took the freshly brewed coffee into the living room. The rest of the evening was spent in jovial companionship and after Mrs. McGantry and Mr. Lee left, Lizzie sat down next to Aunt Dorothy, laid her head on her shoulder and said, "We are truly blessed to have friends that are like family."

"How right you are child," Aunt Dorothy answered.

～

The next few weeks were crammed with pre-wedding preparations and festivities. Lizzie put in extra hours making sure she kept on top of The Biscuit Box responsibilities so the two days before the wedding she could dedicate her attention to preparing the food. She had arranged to have a few of her part-time employees help her set up the day of the wedding and then keep the food trays full so she could be a guest. Aunt Dorothy and Mrs. Wilson had created the center pieces and they were carefully boxed and stored in Mrs. McGantry's garage until the morning of.

~

On Friday morning, Lizzie decided to work on the cake, making a large round and a medium round to build the two tiered cake. She did as much prep as she could for all the other items, as she planned to prepare the day of to ensure that each bite would be fresh. She finished just in time to work out front during the daily rush and after a short lunch break she had returned to the kitchen to begin making the icing that would go on the cake.

She was so intent on what she was doing she hadn't noticed Bennett had stepped into the kitchen and was watching her work. She had just opened a large bag of confectioner's sugar when he spoke, startling her so much the bag flew up out of her hands. As it came down it coated her and a large area around her with white. Bennett could not help himself and doubled over in laughter.

"I ... I ... you scared the stuffing out of me, Bennett! When did you even get here?" Lizzie exclaimed.

Bennett could not answer; his laughter had gone out of control.

"It's not funny!" Lizzie protested but despite her effort to express indignation, she found herself beginning to shake with laughter and before she knew it, she could not stop. Her employees who had been in the front of the store were peeking in the window of the swinging door, but Lizzie did not care. Except for the time she laughed with Mr. Lee on Easter she could not remember the last time she had felt laughter well up from her belly all the way to the tips of her fingers and toes.

"Lizzie you have got to look in the mirror, I now know what you will look like when we are in our eighties," Bennett said between gasps.

Lizzie moved to the bathroom next to her office and peered in the mirror. Her hair was white as snow. Bennett came to stand behind her and handed her a dish towel and with another towel gently tried to help wipe the sugar from the back of her neck and shoulders.

Lizzie, looking at him in the mirror shyly, asked, "So you think you'll know me when we're eighty?"

"I reckon we have known each other since preschool. I can't imagine my life without you in it," he answered without looking up from his task. "I think this is going to take more than dishtowels, let me run you home in my truck. A little sugar won't hurt anything and then once you're cleaned up, I can run you back so you can finish the cake," Bennett offered.

"Okay, let me tell my girls out front," Lizzie answered. When they were on their way, Lizzie asked, "What were you coming by to see me about anyway?"

"I was thinking since you're my date for tomorrow and all, perhaps you would be my date for the rehearsal tonight. My dad made the barbeque and Mr. Lee's brother, Timothy, reserved Gold Bug. Your Aunt Dorothy is already going and I can pick the two of you up," he said.

"I think that would be nice," Lizzie answered trying to keep any indication of excitement out of her voice. He was finally making a move on his own.

Lizzie quickly got cleaned up while Bennett played with the dogs out back. When Bennett dropped her back off at The Biscuit Box, she slid out of the truck and said, "See you tonight."

Bennett waved as she turned to watch him pull away. She walked into a pristine kitchen as her wonderful employees had cleaned up the mess. She found herself unable to stop smiling as she finally made the icing, got it on the cake and got the cake in the walk-in cooler. Now, to find just the right thing to wear for tonight.

Chapter Seventeen

Staring into her closet Lizzie was having a hard time picking out what to wear for the rehearsal. Aunt Dorothy waltzed in wearing a red linen sheath and a coordinating linen fitted jacket.

"Still not dressed?" she asked, walking into Lizzie's closet. After a minute she pulled out a crisp red and white A-line dress with subtle, nautical buttons at the shoulder. Handing it to Lizzie she said, "This with your gold braided sandals would be most appropriate."

Lizzie took the dress and nodded as Aunt Dorothy headed downstairs calling behind her, "Bennett will be here in less than a half hour to collect us, get a move on Lizzie."

Lizzie did as she was told and marveled that as a grown woman Aunt Dorothy still had command over her. She examined herself in the mirror. Aunt Dorothy was right as always. This dress was flattering to her waist, modest enough to be appropriate for the church part of the evening and yet casual enough to not look out of place at a barbeque in the cinder block club house on Gold Bug Island.

She had just made it down the stairs when Bennett pulled up in his SUV. He had on khaki pants, boat shoes and a white button down shirt. He was freshly shaved and smelled faintly of leather mixed with suntan oil. He gallantly escorted Aunt Dorothy to the car and despite her protests seated her in the front passenger seat. Then he opened the back for Lizzie and commented on how nice she looked as he shut her door.

The rehearsal went smoothly and Mrs. McGantry looked radiant in white linen. The party moved on to Gold Bug Island where a fantastic spread of barbeque with all the fixings awaited them. Timothy Lee had also hired a local band and soon many of the guests were shagging to traditional beach music and Lizzie and Bennett joined in as naturally as if they had never been apart. Taking a break, Bennett went off to find some drinks and Lizzie plopped down next to Aunt Dorothy.

"You two certainly look good together, child," Aunt Dorothy commented.

"It certainly feels right," Lizzie responded.

"What, no protest, no reasons it can't be so?" Aunt Dorothy teased.

"No, I will concede maybe you are right about this Aunt Dorothy. I just need time to be sure," she answered.

Bennett returned with drinks and after a short rest, he convinced Aunt Dorothy to join him for a whirl on the dance floor and Lizzie watched them with intense joy. Bennett really was a great guy, good with kids, good with his elders, she had to admit Bennett was also good with her ... who else would put up with her, get her out of scrapes and treat her with respect. But what could she offer him? She felt her self-doubt creeping in to ruin her optimism. *How could I possibly be worthy?* She had to let the thoughts go as Mr. Lee swept her off her feet and onto the dance floor. By the time Bennett had returned Aunt Dorothy and Lizzie back to their door she was too tired to contemplate anymore. She knew she would be getting up early to finish the food for the reception. Aunt Dorothy discreetly entered the house first leaving Lizzie and Bennett alone on the front porch.

They stood together for a moment then Bennett said, "Well, good night, see you tomorrow," and went down the steps, leaving Lizzie standing there wishing he had leaned in to kiss her.

"Good night," she said as under her breath she muttered, "Baby steps, Lizzie, baby steps." As she climbed into bed she heard her phone chirp and she checked the incoming text. It was from Bennett: *Loved shagging with you tonight.* Lizzie texted back: *It was fun, I am looking forward to the wedding.* Lizzie drifted off and to the strains of beach music she shagged with Bennett under a starry sky, the dreams carrying her through to morning.

~

As the alarm went off, Lizzie groaned. It was still dark outside. The dogs, however, were eager to start their day, wagging their tails and licking her legs as they were sticking out from under the sheets. She dragged herself up, pulled on some jeans and a t-shirt and took the dogs out to the backyard.

Now that she was up, she felt the butterflies stir deep within her belly. Her first catering event and another date with Bennett. At least she counted the previous evening as a date. She hoped Bennett viewed it that way as well. When she returned to the kitchen, she was surprised to see Aunt Dorothy already up and waiting with a travel mug full of coffee and a bag with a blueberry muffin ready to go.

"Thought this would help you get out the door faster," she said.

"Thanks!" Lizzie said. "I will be back around twelve-thirty to take a quick shower and change." She grabbed her keys and purse.

At The Biscuit Box she was grateful she had taken the time to do so much prep work the day before and quickly got to work preparing everything that could be made ahead of time. Lizzie was in her element; the ovens were on, the stand mixer whirred and pots of water were rising to a boil on the range. Lizzie had carefully written a timetable to follow and so far she was slightly ahead.

She had chilled all the ingredients for the St. Cecilia's punch, a special request from Mr. Lee who remembered his maternal grandmother making the punch for nearly every special occasion. This of course had horrified the majority of the Lee clan, as they were strict Baptists. Mr. Lee's maternal grandmother was Episcopalian and according to Mr. Lee was amused at the discomfort of her son-in-law's family.

She had sent Laura over to the church with the first load of food, giving her detailed instructions on where to put everything once she unloaded. Lizzie was going to finish up the prep work and then have Laura transport all that was left but the cake. Lizzie wanted to transport the cake. She was the most nervous about her first wedding cake. Zoe was going to meet her at the church kitchen to cook the shrimp at the last minute to go on the shrimp and grits station and also to oversee the servers so Lizzie could enjoy the event. The florist was bringing the flowers for the cake directly to the church, so around eleven-thirty Lizzie carefully transported the cake and all the various serving trays and equipment over to the church.

The church was blessed to have a large commercial refrigerator and once Lizzie had decorated the cake with the flowers, she was able to put it in to keep it as fresh as possible. After another trip to collect the punch ingredients and a few more supplies she returned to the church.

She set out the serving trays on the buffet tables in the parish hall labeling each with a sticky note so the hired servers and Zoe would know what needed to go where once it was time. Lizzie went over her list and schedule multiple times, terrified she had forgotten something. Not only was this a professional growth opportunity, it was for friends and family. She wanted it to be perfect.

Zoe arrived, taking over and shooing her off to go and get cleaned up. It was one o'clock by the time Lizzie pulled up at the house and Aunt Dorothy met her at the door. "I was beginning to worry," she said.

"Sorry, I got caught up in details. Zoe had to shoo me away," Lizzie said. "I'll be ready fast."

"Hurry, child, we need to leave here at two," Aunt Dorothy said.

Lizzie bounded up the steps and returned five minutes before two, looking stunning in a green silk dress with a V-neck and fluttery cap sleeves. It nipped in at the waist and draped perfectly, with the hem landing just above her knees. She wore her favorite Stuart Weitzman gold strappy backless heels with a delicate bow detail. Her emerald green necklace, ring and tear drop earrings finished the look and her hair was swept up in an elegant up-do, a few tendrils escaping around her face.

"You look stunning," Aunt Dorothy exclaimed.

"You look stunning yourself," Lizzie answered as she took in Aunt Dorothy, a vision in an elegant navy raw silk ensemble and classic pearl jewelry. As the attendant to the bride she would also have a small bouquet of white roses she would carry for the ceremony.

"I would have thought I had outgrown my bridesmaid days," Aunt Dorothy laughed.

"I don't think there is a cut-off age," Lizzie replied. "I suppose we should get a move on," Lizzie added.

"No dear, slight change of plans. Bennett is picking us up, ah, here he is now," Aunt Dorothy said and she headed out the door.

Lizzie followed and felt her heart flutter up in her throat as she took in Bennett in his white trousers and double breasted blue blazer, although he could be standing there in a torn t-shirt and board shorts and she would probably have the same reaction. He had on his sunglasses so she could not tell his initial reaction to her, but noted his lingering hand on her back as he escorted her to the car.

Bennett handled his job of escorting the bride down the aisle like a pro and got a few laughs as he admonished Mr. Lee to take good care of his girl. The ceremony was touching with Mrs. McGantry and Mr. Lee exchanging vows they wrote themselves. Not a dry eye was among those gathered in the pews as Reverend Truett pronounced the couple Mr. and Mrs. Thomas Eugene Lee and the two exchanged a passionate kiss.

The guests followed the happy couple out of the church and directly into the receiving line before entering the parish hall that was transformed into an elegantly appointed nautical themed venue. The flowers were all white with small touches of silver that popped against the navy blue linen that was trimmed with crisp white ribbon. The food display was inviting and Lizzie felt a burst of pride as she watched her servers fan out with trays of small bites to tempt the guests. It was hard for her not to head to the kitchen and pitch in.

A small quartet played classical music in one corner and a well-appointed bar was set up in the other, which might have horrified Mr. Lee's Baptist relatives, at least the older ones, but seemed natural for the friends and family of the new Mrs. Lee as they were primarily Episcopal. *Mr. Lee's grandmother would be pleased*, thought Lizzie.

Guest after guest found their way to Lizzie, singing the praises of her food and the beauty of the cake. Bennett brought both her and Aunt Dorothy drinks and plates of food and the three sat together watching the crowd. Mr. and Mrs. Lee came over. Mrs. Lee said, "Lizzie, you surpassed our expectations. We have heard rave after rave about the food."

"All in a day's work," Lizzie smiled at the happy couple.

"So, where are you two headed for your honeymoon?" Bennett asked.

"We are off to exotic Antigua but we are staying tonight at the inn at Two Meeting Street," answered Mr. Lee.

"Sounds romantic doesn't it?" chimed in Aunt Dorothy. "By the way, I have put your bag in the limo so you are set to go."

"Thank you so much, Dorothy," Mrs. Lee said. "I suppose we better move on to cut the cake," she added.

They watched as the two moved to the cake table and a crowd gathered around. Bennett headed back to the bar for a refill and after a while Lizzie became aware that he had not returned. She scanned the hall and saw him talking with a vivacious brunette who was laughing at whatever he was saying and her eyes narrowed as Lizzie noticed she kept putting her hand on Bennett's arm in a very familiar way. He was obviously enjoying himself and Lizzie's self-doubt came back in full force. *He will probably end up with her and they will have beautiful children who wear coordinating smocked dresses*, she thought.

"Who is that talking with Bennett?" she asked.

"That is Vivian, Mr. Lee's niece from Cheraw. His sister's daughter. She dated Bennett a few summers ago when she did an internship in Tommy's office," Aunt Dorothy answered.

Lizzie felt her face turn hot. She had not realized she had asked the question out loud. But now that she realized Aunt Dorothy was in the know, she pressed her for more information.

"So she's an attorney? How serious were they? Does she live here?" She rapidly fired off the questions that were swirling around in her brain.

"Yes, not particularly and I believe she is back in Cheraw in her own law practice," Aunt Dorothy replied. "Anything else your inquisitive mind is wondering about?"

"No ma'am," Lizzie answered uncomfortably. "How about if I fetch us some cake?" Without waiting for an answer, Lizzie got up and moved across the hall to the cake table.

Mrs. Wilson came in from her left and gave her a side hug, "Lizzie, this cake is remarkable! This is the best food I have had at an event in years! Would you consider handling my mother's one hundredth birthday party this fall?"

"Of course I would. Nana Gowdy is dear to my heart," Lizzie answered and to herself thought, *I bet Vivian doesn't even know Nana Gowdy.*

Lizzie collected the cake and a few more compliments and as she returned to the table she was pleased to see Bennett had rejoined them, minus the lovely Vivian. But she threw up a wall of defense mostly out of reflex and after dropping off the cake, pretended to check in with her staff and visit with other acquaintances around the room.

She carefully packed a special basket with samplings from the food table and a generous piece of cake and stowed it with the bags already in the limo. Shortly after, Amy's children circulated among the guests handing out bubbles to blow at the happy couple when they made their escape to the suite awaiting them downtown.

When the newlyweds finally made their departure, the guests lingered, not wanting an end to the reception and soon many were making plans to carry the party to a new location. Bennett approached and asked if she was ready to go.

"Um, would you mind taking Aunt Dorothy home? I want to help my staff wrap things up here and get every thing back to The Biscuit Box," she explained, aware that Bennett was studying her intensely with his piercing eyes.

She glanced at him momentarily then settled her eyes on the floor. He stared at her for what seemed to be a long time, and then finally responded. "Sure, okay." Without another word, he headed over to collect Aunt Dorothy.

Bennett headed out to pull the car up. Before Aunt Dorothy followed him out, she swung by where Lizzie was standing and made herself busy with packing up supplies.

Aunt Dorothy leaned in close and said, "I would say your jealousy is matching the green of your frock, child. I would rethink the path you just put yourself on." Then without another word, she kissed Lizzie on the forehead and walked away.

Lizzie felt tears well up in her eyes, but she blinked them away. Grabbing an apron, she put it on to protect her dress and put herself in work mode. It was well after ten when she had finished, transporting, cleaning and putting away all the things she had hauled over to the church. Well, at least there wasn't any food to bring back. The guests had consumed most of it and out of what little was left, she had packed an assortment for the newlyweds. She had let the servers polish off the rest of it as they cleaned up.

When she finally got home, Aunt Dorothy had gone to bed. Lizzie was relieved as she had been bracing herself for a lecture on how she had treated Bennett. How different she felt from twenty-four hours before. After the rehearsal, she had been sure she and Bennett would slip right into romance at the wedding. Instead, she was sure she had ruined her last chance. Her sleep was not restful as she tossed and turned and dreamed of Bennett dancing away from her with Vivian.

Chapter Eighteen

A few weeks had passed and Lizzie had not heard from Bennett. He hadn't even made his usual stops by The Biscuit Box. Lizzie felt herself sinking like a stone in the pluff mud. She had screwed things up again.

One evening Aunt Dorothy quietly patted her hand across the table and said, "Lizzie, inertia will get you nowhere. Only you can fix this and you need to do so soon, for both our sakes."

She had graciously given Lizzie space since the wedding and had not inquired how things stood with Bennett. Now Aunt Dorothy was stepping in. She knew Lizzie had slid from contemplation to defeatism. Lizzie smiled back at her weakly and felt the tears begin to slide down her cheeks. Before she knew it she was wracked with sobs and Aunt Dorothy had moved around behind her enveloping her with her embrace. Once she had cried herself out, she sat up and said, "I need to come up with a plan."

"Yes, you do child, yes you do," Aunt Dorothy replied.

Lizzie mulled it over for a few more days and then called Amy and M.A. to arrange a girl's night out. She needed to run her idea past her confidants and get any inside information Amy might have that would help her in her endeavor to win Bennett back once and for all.

～

Friday night the three friends met on the deck of one of their favorite beachside bars. It overlooked the volleyball nets on the Isle of Palms and Lizzie spilled her guts about her true feelings and the plan she was formulating to win Bennett's heart.

"So, what do you think?" she asked.

"Well I think you have his heart already. It's his mind you need to convince. I think he is unsure he can have your heart—that is what you need to convey to him," Amy thoughtfully responded.

"I think the food part is a no brainer. Who can resist your cooking?" M.A. added.

"So, do you think he will come?" Lizzie asked.

"I know he will come. He is like a moth to a flame where you are concerned," Amy answered.

"Gee, thanks," Lizzie said.

"I don't mean you're destructive. I just mean he can't resist you," Amy explained, laying a hand on her arm reassuringly.

"You're sure he has no interest in that Vivian or anyone else?" she probed.

"Absolutely not," Amy insisted. "He was never serious about Vivian, and there is no one else," she reassured Lizzie.

"Now you better move on this plan soon. I want to make you my sister-in-law as soon as possible," Amy added.

"Plus, I want a chance to be part of a wedding where the groom actually likes me," M.A. exclaimed.

"Thanks, girls. I don't know what I would do without you," Lizzie said. The three friends finished their drinks and looked out over the sand to the waves as the sunlight faded into dusk.

～

She selected Saturday as the night to implement the plan. That way, if it was a disaster, she could hide in her bed on Sunday to recover. She had gone home from The Biscuit Box at noon to shower and change. She had put on her white capri pants and her signature green halter top. She went back half an hour before closing time and sent her employees home, telling them she was going to close up.

She carefully dressed a table for two in the center of the dining room, complete with candles. In the kitchen, she began preparing a special meal, all of Bennett's favorites—pan-fried flounder with a brown butter sauce, Carolina gold rice and a dark leafy green salad with homemade vinaigrette. She had planned his favorite apple pie for dessert, and would serve it with homemade ice cream.

She put the pie in the oven, the rice in the steamer and got the fish ready to go in the pan. Knowing, via Amy, he was finishing up on one of his charter boats, she called.

"Hello," Bennett said.

"Hey, Bennett. It's me," Lizzie heard herself say lamely.

"I know. Your name shows up with your number," Bennett said.

"Um ... I hate to bother you. I know you are not my landlord any more, but I am having a little trouble with what I suspect is a leak. Any chance you can swing by and take a look?" she asked.

"Uh, yeah, I am about to leave from the marina, so I should be there in about twenty or so."

"Great. I left the front door unlocked, so just come on in. I might be back in the office when you get here," she said, pleased her ploy had worked.

"Okay, see you in a few," he said, and hung up.

Lizzie felt panic wash over her. She rushed back to the front to light the candles on the table and placed a card with his name on the plate closest to the door. She hurried back to the kitchen and peeked in at the pie. It was beginning to get a golden hue on the crust but not quite set in the middle. She put some oil and butter in a pan and turned on the burner. Lizzie decided to put the exhaust fan on as well. She did not want a fishy smell to take over the kitchen.

The salad! Lizzie flew to the walk-in cooler and yanked on the old ornery handle and walked in to gather the greens for the salad. She stood for a moment enjoying the effect the cool air was having on her composure. She scanned the shelves to see if there were any other ingredients she needed. Satisfied she had what she needed, she pushed on the release handle on the inside of the door. It fell right through the door and clattered onto the kitchen floor.

Lizzie froze in shock. She was shut in the cooler! Her mind raced as she looked around for anything she might use to help her get the door open. Setting down the greens, she threw her weight against the door. That only resulted in a bruised shoulder. She looked for something to put down into the door mechanism, but the best she could find was a twisty tie that had been around the greens. She straightened it out and attempted to use it to catch the latch, but after a few unsuccessful attempts, it slipped from her hand and disappeared down into the inner cavity of the door.

She felt herself begin to shiver from the cold. Through the hole where the handle used to be, she could hear the pan with the oil and butter sizzling. *Great,* she thought. *I can see the headline now, 'Love Sick Woman Freezes to Death in Fire.'* Surely Bennett would be here soon. He'd see what a disaster she truly was and walk away from her forever! *Get a grip, Lizzie, you can get yourself out of this.*

Unbeknownst to her, Bennett had just entered the front of the building and taken in the table set for two. He began reading the heartfelt declaration Lizzie had written out, because she knew she wouldn't have the guts to say it.

Dear Bennett,
Sorry does not seem adequate enough a word to say. I wronged
you all those years ago, when I misjudged you. In the past year,
I have wronged you more times than I can count. The truth
is, I have been afraid to admit to myself, and to you, that I
am still in love with you. You have demonstrated time and
time again that you are a man of integrity and honor. I don't
deserve you. If you would give me another chance, I want to
become the woman you can be proud to call your own. If there
is even an inkling that we have a chance, please sit down and
pour the wine. I will join you soon with a meal I hope you will
never forget.
Love, Lizzie

Bennett sat down. He could hear clanging sounds coming from the kitchen and he smiled. He poured the wine into the two glasses on the table. In the kitchen the pan on the stove had reached rock melting temperatures and the smoke, despite the efforts of the exhaust fan, finally set off the fire alarm.

Bennett burst in the kitchen, looked around wildly, and quickly spotted the pan. Grabbing the fire extinguisher hanging on the wall, he quickly put out the grease fire that had begun and turned off the stove. He looked around and began to worry when he did not see Lizzie.

"Lizzie?" he called.

Lizzie weakly called back, "I'm in the cooler."

The exhaust fan made it too hard for Bennett to hear her so he called again, looking in the office and bathroom. He called louder, then again. Finally he walked over and turning off the exhaust fan. He heard a faint voice and his eyes settled on the broken cooler handle lying on the floor. Rushing over, he peered in the hole and their eyes met. "Hold on, Lizzie, I'll get you out! I have some tools in the truck." He dashed out front and came back seconds later with his tool box.

He located what he needed and took the door right off the hinges and scooped her up in his arms. She shivered uncontrollably and he vigorously rubbed her arms and back trying to encourage the blood flow.

"What the hell happened?" Bennett demanded.

"It's that dumb cooler handle. I've been meaning to get it looked at. Tonight when I tried to leave the cooler, the whole dumb thing fell out," Lizzie answered, shivering with every syllable.

He held her close and gradually her shivering subsided. "So you thought I could be reeled in with romance and flounder," he said as he spotted the fish on the cutting board. Unfortunately, it was covered with flame retardant from the extinguisher.

"I was hoping so," Lizzie answered meekly, not daring to look at him.

He continued to hold her tight. She did not make any effort to move away as they stood in silence for a few moments.

"I believe the fire department should be arriving any second," Bennett said. "Your security system would have alerted them. Most likely they've sent someone to check things out."

"Oh, I hadn't thought about that," Lizzie said, still not wanting to move out of his arms.

"I read your letter," Bennett offered.

"Oh, and what did you think?" Lizzie asked as she peered up at him.

"Lizzie, I have loved you since we were four years old. You have had my heart all these years. That will never change. You already are the woman I would be proud to call my own. My question to you is do really feel the same? Or ... is this just a rebound from your failed marriage?"

Lizzie stepped back and looked directly at him. "Yes, I feel the same. I have loved you for as long as I can remember, and I will love you for always." She was trembling now, but from emotion, not the cold.

"Are you sure?" he pressed.

"Yes," she said, not breaking eye contact. "How do you know you're sure?" he asked.

Without skipping a beat she said, "As Aunt Dorothy would say, 'the eyes have it.'" With that, Bennett saw all he needed in those emerald green eyes staring into his. As the siren's wail came closer, he pulled her to him and kissed her.

Book Club
Question Guide

1. Which character, or characters did you most connect with, and why?

2. How does Lizzie change in the course of the book and what traits stayed the same?

3. What other characters did you see transformation in?

4. What theme or themes, was the author trying to convey in the telling of this story?

5. Do you think Aunt Dorothy was right to leave Lizzie while she was still floundering? Why or why not?

6. How does the the focus on the setting add or detreact to the story?

7. Why do you think Lizzie is so determined to think the worst of Bennett?

8. What emotions were evoked in you as you read?

9. At what point in the story did you decide if you liked the book or not? What helped you make that decision?

10. If you could ask the author any question what would it be?

About the Author

Author Julie Allan grew up an army brat, living a nomadic lifestyle until she landed in Charleston, South Carolina as a teenager. Now, her thirty-year love affair with the Carolina Lowcountry inspires her tales of spirited women that you'll want to call friends. When she is not teaching elementary school or writing, you can find Julie at the beach, in the garden or hanging out with her beloved golden retrievers.

In addition to *The Eyes Have It*, Julie has three forthcoming Lowcountry novels. *The Heart Knows It* is scheduled for release in the fall of 2016. *The Soul Believes It* and *Pearls of Wisdom* will be released in 2017.

You can connect with author Julie Allan via her website, <u>authorjulieallan.com</u>, and on Twitter and Facebook. Reviews are always welcome and appreciated.

CPSIA information can be obtained
at www.ICGtesting.com
Printed in the USA
LVOW08s0923050217
523244LV00003B/552/P